CLAMP DOWN!

Tag checked his radar screen again and found that the two blips he had seen earlier were returning in the direction from which they came. With a few quick strokes he calculated the speed and direction of the aircraft to give himself a good idea of where they had been. Yeshev was headed right for the spot.

Even through the deep snow, the two tanks covered the ten kilometers that they had to travel in less than fifteen minutes. The two hundred Chinese paratroopers were still trying to group up in the open when Tag and Yeshev brought their machines into positions overlooking the drop zone.

Yeshev said over the radio, "Take them."

"Load HE," Tag said. "Forward at a trot."

The 120mm roared, echoed by Yeshev's gun, while Tag and Giesla opened up with their coax machine guns and Fruits alternately fed the 120mm and let off micro-second bursts from the 37mm Phalanx.

With the two tanks moving on them fast from different quarters, the Chinese never had a chance . . .

TANKWAR V:

FIREFIGHT

TANKWAR V:
FIREFIGHT

LARRY STEELBAUGH

BERKLEY BOOKS, NEW YORK

TANKWAR V: FIREFIGHT

A Berkley Book / published by arrangement with
the author

PRINTING HISTORY
Berkley edition / February 1992

ISBN: 0-425-13232-3

A BERKLEY BOOK ® TM 757, 375
Berkley Books are published by The Berkley Publishing Group,
200 Madison Avenue, New York, New York 10016.
The name "Berkley" and the "B" logo
are trademarks belonging to Berkley Publishing Corporation.

PRINTED IN THE UNITED STATES OF AMERICA

10 9 8 7 6 5 4 3 2 1

For my friends and colleagues
who died with their dreams
on the streets of Beijing

1

Moonlight filtered through the thatched walls, and Tag could hear the wash of the surf on the beach, see, if he turned to look out the opened shutters, the play of stars on the water. But Giesla glowed in the pale light, and she was all his eyes sought. He sat on the edge of the king-size bed that took up most of the bedroom in the cabana on the beach at Molokai, and he looked at her in silence. The light seemed not to fall on her but to come from within, like the aura of a saint in a painting by an Old Master, but Giesla was not posed for beatification. She lay naked on a sprawl of pillows, rolled half on her side, one arm lying languidly along her hip, her hair thrown back and fanned against the sheets. Tag could see the wet motion of her tongue gliding across her lips, the shadows of her nipples as she touched them in the dark. He dropped the towel that he had carried from the shower, rolled onto his belly, stretched across the bed, and cupped the hollow behind Giesla's knee.

"Have I," he asked, "delivered on my promise of a bed?"

"And this one," she said, "is the best yet. This is where I want to stay always, Max. It is as though we are the only people on earth."

Tag knew what she really meant. What she meant was that it was as though they were different people, that they were not soldiers, that they had not just come through war in

1

Europe, through the nuclear devastation of much of southern Germany, that they were just a man and a woman fallen
deep inside themselves, back in touch with something pri-
mal and unalloyed, a sustaining something that they had
hoarded, the way family silver, art works, and rare manu-
scripts are kept hidden until an invading army passes.

Like many others who fought with them, Tag and Giesla
had themselves been left as scorched earth, emotionally
seared, and like the family digging up its treasure when
the army has gone, they doled out their store of affection as
though fearful the war might return and take it from them.
Their love had had its birth and genesis in the smithy of
war, was tempered and annealed by it, and when the war
was over, each of them had wondered whether their love
would be too brittle to survive the peace.

Throughout the weeks immediately following the end,
while they went through the motions of demobilization,
debriefing, and emotional decompression, neither Tag nor
Giesla had had time to dwell long on their apprehensions.
But once they had been granted their extended leaves, passed through the obligatory parades and awards ceremonies,
and begun the tour Tag had planned for Giesla across the
United States, their fears had risen between them. In city
after city, in hotel after hotel, where identical philodendra
dripped from similar atria above indistinguishable lobbies,
they had failed to recapture the depth and intensity of feeling that they had known under the cloud of war. Only here,
after nearly a week of rolling surf, limpid lagoons, and
tropical mountain forest where transplanted European deer
howl at night, had they begun to reclaim the passion and
deep, easy familiarity that had supported them through the
war.

"We are," Tag said. "We are the first, last, and only
ones."

He pulled himself on his elbows across the bed, lift-
ing his hips to ease the drag on his swelling erection, and

slid his hand up the back of Giesla's thigh, over her hip, and into the hollow at the small of her back, drawing his head level with her breasts. He kissed the dark shadows of her nipples and said, "We shouldn't waste our first-best bed."

Giesla drew a breath between her teeth and slipped lazily into his arms, bringing Tag's face to hers. She kissed him with her lips and tongue, biting and sucking, her hands making a slow search of the scars on his back, his shoulder, his ribs. She felt the hard planes of his ass, spread her fingers over it, and brought him closer so she could feel the thickness of his cock against her belly. Then she reached between them and took that swelling cock in her hand, pressing it against her as she rubbed its length and moved her hips in slow undulations.

Tag lifted her leg and Giesla maneuvered him inside her and they lay there on their sides, each looking deep into the other's face, hardly moving, at first. Tag thrust harder, and Giesla took a sharp breath, pressing down against him. and then they began to search each other, rolling onto his back and hers, feeling a red-tinted pleasure being to grow, fusing, melding them. They came together as though both their hearts would burst.

Giesla wiped a long strand of her blond hair from the corner of her mouth and kissed Tag's cheek that was lying against her own. She hugged the thick barrel of his chest and let a ripple of relief and joy pass through her, sending a sexual tingle to her toes.

"What?" Tag said softly in her ear.

"I feel I have been put all back together," she said, "that I have rediscovered myself . . . and you."

Tag mumbled something about being field-stripped, oiled, and assembled.

"You are such a sweet-talking man, Max Tag," said Giesla. "But I forgive you, because you are such a good fuck. And sometimes a dumb one."

Tag raised himself on one elbow. "I'm sorry," he said. "I guess I just wanted to forget that things came between us for a while, didn't want to even acknowledge it, really. We're not going to fight now, are we, now that we're back?"

Giesla locked Tag's hips between her knees and flipped him on his back, surprising him, as she always did, with the strength concealed in her centerfold figure.

"Yes," she said, smiling mischievously as a light breeze rippled moonlight through the thatch walls and across her face. "Now I am going to really punish you."

She tossed her long hair forward over one shoulder and switched it across his chest.

"Oh, no," Tag said. "Not the brier patch."

Early the next morning, Tag and Giesla ran on the beach, swam, made love again, and showered, before they walked to the little restaurant set in a grove of palms for breakfast. They had become favorites of the Chinese family who operated the restaurant, especially the teenage son, Young Li, whose infatuation with Giesla was elaborately obvious and unabashed. Whenever they came in, Young Li would leave whatever he was doing to greet them and walk next to Giesla as he showed them to a table, holding her chair when she sat and beaming at the world. Old Li, the boy's father, would often scowl at him from the open kitchen where he cooked, but then would smile and wink at Tag.

This morning, however, when Young Li met them at the door, he was subdued, almost somber.

"Good morning," he said, his arms stiff at his sides.

"Good morning," said Tag and Giesla happily. But when Tag stepped aside for Young Li to be next to Giesla, the boy did not move.

"Any table you like," Young Li said. He turned toward the kitchen, adding, "I will get your coffee."

Young Li served them in almost total silence, muttering monosyllables in response to their questions. Tag and

Giesla talked about it over their bread, fruit, and the special rice *congee*—a sweet gruel that Old Li made with coconut milk and pickled melon—until Giesla at last said, "I think he is only sad and maybe a little jealous."

"A little late for jealousy, isn't it?" said Tag.

"Not of you," Giesla replied. "He is jealous that we are going off somewhere, while he has to stay here."

"Impatient with paradise, huh?" Tag said. "I guess that would make you sad or something. Suppose we can do anything?"

"Wait here," she said.

Giesla walked across the airy dining room, only now beginning to fill with the tourists from the other cabanas, and fished in the pocket of her baggy shorts for the disc of Soviet lapel brass that had become her worry stone. She did not recall how she came to have it—taken from one of the several prisoners she had interrogated, no doubt—but she felt her need for it was past now, and it was all she had at hand to give Young Li, who was standing glumly behind the counter that separated the dining room from the kitchen.

"Li," she said to him, "you know that Max and I must leave today"—Young Li nodded—"but before we go, I wanted to tell you something. You and your family have been very kind to us, and we have become very fond of you—especially of you—and I want you to remember me, with this."

She opened her hand and showed him the round bit of embossed brass.

"Take it," she said. "Please. It has been luck for me, and I want you to have it now."

Young Li looked up at her and flushed, but he took the brass, held it between his thumb and middle finger, and looked at it. Giesla kissed him on each cheek before he could speak.

"Thank you for accepting it," she said. "I think we will have one more cup of coffee."

When Young Li brought the coffee, he had on the tray two small, silk-covered boxes latched with bone pins. After he poured the coffee, Young Li put the tray on an empty table nearby and set the boxes in front of Tag and Giesla.

"My family," he said, his tone very correct, "has been honored to have you as our guests, and we humbly hope you will accept these small tokens of our regard."

"Thank you," Tag said, pushing back the pin to unlatch one of the boxes. "Thank you very much."

Inside the boxes were nestled identical painted wooden cranes, one leg bent, necks extended, their red-crowned heads cocked to one side.

"The crane," Young Li said, as he removed them from their boxes, "is a symbol in China of longevity and faithfulness, for when cranes mate they mate for life."

With this Young Li turned the cranes to face each other, made a quick movement with his hands, and sat them on the table, now twined together at their bent legs and necks.

Giesla picked up the cranes, separated them, and laced them together again.

Tag felt uncomfortably like a groom, and Young Li hovered over them officious as a marriage broker.

Tag and Giesla had lunch on the deck of the big island catamaran that took them back to Maui, where they caught a plane for the mainland. They spent the night in San Francisco, complete with a romantic dinner on Fishermen's Wharf, and the next morning, Christmas Eve, flew to Montana and the ranch where Tag had grown up. Fruits Tutti and Ham Jefferson—respectively, the loader and gunner on the XM-F4 tank No Slack Too—would be meeting them there on the thirtieth, and they would all spend New Year together, before reporting back for transport to Belgium and a much-anticipated meeting with General Ross Kettle, the Allies' supreme commander in Europe during the late war.

Kate, Tag's mother, and his father, Otto, both fell for Giesla, and his brother, Fred, usually marked by his patient intelligence and quiet mien, acted the absolute sport around her, not entirely to the pleasure of his wife, Marie.

Christmas morning Tag and Giesla awoke twined together like the cranes Young Li had given them, cramped on one of the two single beds in the room that Max and Fred had shared as boys. Tag knew that his mother's putting them here had been a sort of compromise—letting them share a room while pretending they would sleep in separate beds—and Giesla had absolutely refused to let him move the beds together. Now, she slid from beneath the covers, hop-stepped across the chilly room to the other bed, and threw herself beneath the sheets, shivering uncontrollably.

"What the hell are you doing?" Tag asked.

"I do not want your mother to think I am some kind of tramp," Giesla said through her chattering teeth.

Then she was up and out of bed again and pulling on her clothes. "Now," she said, "I am going down to help her with the breakfast. You make the beds and stay here until you are called."

"Yes, *ma'am*," Tag said. He rolled over, pulled the blankets over his head, and mumbled from beneath them, "I like my eggs over easy."

His father was just returning from the feedlot when Tag came down to breakfast, and Kate, Giesla, and Marie were pulling biscuits from the oven, layering slabs of ham on a platter, mixing orange juice, and draining fried eggs on a brown paper sack, working efficiently as a submarine crew. Tag poured coffee for himself, his father, and Fred, and soon everyone sat down to a steaming country meal.

After they had cleared the breakfast dishes, they went into the living room, where a big, decorated spruce stood in one corner surrounded by brightly wrapped boxes. Otto Tag sat a blue enamel pot of coffee on the fender of the fireplace and, as was the tradition in his house, passed out the presents one at a time, to be opened and admired by everyone before the next one was handed over. There were sweaters and gloves and perfumes and boxer shorts with blue whales on them, and from Ross Kettle two unexpected, autographed copies of his book *Armor Tomorrow* for Tag and Giesla. Also for her, Tag had a necklace of gold and three kinds of coral that he had bought at a shop in Lahaina on Maui. For him, she had a simple, heavy platinum ring with the stylized nose of a tank as its set.

It was midmorning before the unwrapping ceremony was done, and Tag, Giesla, Fred, and Marie wore new scarves, hats, and gloves when they trooped together toward the horse barn behind the house, their breath hanging thinly in the still, cold, sun-shot air.

"This," Fred said, "is what I've been waiting to show you, Max. Wait here."

Fred went into the barn and in a minute came back into the corral leading a handsome chestnut stallion by the halter. He walked the horse over to the others, where it pawed a time or two and tossed its head, then sniffed at the people like a dog.

"This is Blade," said Fred. "Merry Christmas, brother."

"My God, Fred," Tag said, stroking the stallion's neck, "this is not your basic cow pony. Did you steal him?"

"Max!" Giesla said, not entirely attuned to the forms of affection that obtained between the brothers.

Fred squeezed Giesla's shoulders—while Marie knit her brow—and said, "Damn near. A thoroughbred trainer I know brought him to me with pneumonia. I saved him, but there was some scarring on his lungs—not bad, but enough to keep him off the track. The owner just gave him to me for the fees."

"But what am I gonna do with him, Fred?" Max said.

"Breed him to my mares," his brother replied. "I figure that by the time you get out of the Army, we'll have a pretty good breeding operation going. And you'll owe me, oh, about a million dollars for keeping it up for you."

Tag pulled his brother away from Giesla and hugged him. "You're all heart, Freddy," he said. "Thanks."

"Well," Marie said, "are we going to neck or are we going to ride?"

Giesla stood back while the others saddled Blade and three other horses, saying nothing and eyeing the entire operation apprehensively.

As Fred and Marie led their horses out of the barn, Giesla said to Tag, who was handing her the reins to a dappled mare, "Max, perhaps I should not go."

"Not go? Why?" he asked.

Giesla looked angrily off to one side. "Damn you, Max Tag," she said. "I do not know how to ride the horse."

Seeing how angry and frustrated she was, Tag bit his tongue to keep from laughing aloud. With some coaxing he got her in the saddle, where she sat grim-faced and uneasy as the four of them let the horses amble out of the corral and across the rolling country toward the tree line that marked the banks of the Teton River. Despite her apprehensions, Giesla relaxed enough on the ride to appreciate the scenery and realize why Max loved this country so much. The sky seemed immense and immensely blue, faintly striated with high, wispy clouds, and to the west, on the horizon, rose the sawtooth peaks of the Montana Rockies. Nowhere in Europe had she ever experienced such vastness. The plains of Africa that she had known were old, exhausted lands compared to this. She sensed the youth and expansiveness that she had long associated with Americans, with Tag, and felt she knew now that it came from the very shape of their land.

Over the next five days, after Fred and Marie had returned to their home in Great Falls, Tag and Giesla enjoyed another episode of profound intimacy, much as they had in the tropical embrace of Hawaii. Here, the cold invigorated them, and Giesla proved a quick study at horsemanship.

She was delighted by the small herd of buffalo that Otto let roam his acres, and once she and Tag saw elk grazing with the cattle in a far pasture. On the thirtieth, however, when they drove into Great Falls to pick up Ham and Fruits at the airport, despite being happy to see their crewmen, Tag and Giesla knew that their idyll was coming to an end.

The following evening, New Year's Eve, there was a big party at the Tag ranch, with neighbors and friends coming from all over the county to see Max and meet Giesla and the two men who had gone through the war with them. Kate Tag, being from Missouri, insisted on having black-eyed peas, corn bread, and fried hog jowl for everyone to eat at midnight, to insure luck for the coming year.

Ham Jefferson, fortified by several cups of Kate's eggnog punch, said to her as he sopped up pot liquor with a wedge of corn bread, "Miz Tag, it's a real delight to know that civilization came west with you. My mama was worried sick that I wouldn't get my jowl meat and peas for New Year."

Tag, standing nearby, said, "Oh, Mom, I was afraid of this. Be careful he doesn't try to get himself adopted."

Kate Tag beamed.

Later, when the crowd had thinned, Tag sat with his father, Fruits, and Ham around the fire, finishing the last of the eggnog. Otto Tag said, "Well, boys, any idea where you'll be next—after you report back to Germany, I mean?"

"I don't know that it will be Germany, Dad," said Tag. "We're all supposed to report as a unit back to General Kettle in Brussels, that's all I know for sure."

"Yeah," Fruits Tutti said, "at least it ain't to Siberia. Dat's some bad news comin' down out dere."

"That's Mongolia, Fruit Loops," Ham said, "and that is Ivan's own little problem."

"Yeah, Dad," Tag said, "I imagine that Kettle has some cushy R and D thing for us, maybe a little training gig. He's kept us under NATO command to keep us together, so we're not looking at staff positions or anything like that, but I think the general's going to let us slide for a while."

One week later, on a raw, wet day in Belgium, Tag was shown into General Ross Kettle's private office at NATO headquarters in Brussels. It was just as Tag remembered it from his previous visit there, the one during which Kettle had ordered him to deploy the No Slack Too behind the Warsaw Pact lines. Nothing seemed to have changed in the office. The small statue of many-handed Shiva still stood on the table by the door, the air was still redolent with the smells of books and leather chairs and pipe tobacco, and Ross Kettle was again poring over a dossier on the desk before him. Later Tag would wonder why he ever thought that things might be different this time.

"Sit down, Max," Ross Kettle said, standing to return Tag's salute. "Help yourself to coffee." The general indicated a steel vacuum bottle and two porcelain cups on a tray on the edge of his desk.

While Tag sat and poured, Kettle walked along the book-lined wall, as though looking for a title, then turned abruptly and came back to his chair.

"Been keeping up with the news, Max?"

"Just the weather and sports, sir," Tag said.

"Well, what I'm going to tell you hasn't been much publicized, anyway. You want a little insight on how the wheels of world power turn, Max?"

"I'm all ears, sir."

Kettle picked a gnarled briar pipe from the rack of them on his desk and began rubbing its bowl with his thumb. "Max, what has happened within the Soviet Union is nothing short of astounding, even more so than the way history has repeated itself in the rest of Europe. Communism is dead on this continent, Max, at least the totalitarian Marxist-Leninist variety. We crippled it—you and I and hundreds of thousands of other soldiers—but it was the people of the

Russian Republic, a couple of very brave Soviet generals, and some few sane savvy politicians within the Kremlin who really brought the beast down. I've been to Moscow since I last saw you, Max, and I can say that no one even suspected the atmosphere of change we witnessed there. The Svetlovists, you see, never gave up. When their economic policies lost favor and they had to go essentially underground as the hard-liners regained power, they continued to critique their programs, refine their economic philosophy, and it led them closer and closer to the West. That they were able to mastermind and accomplish a *coup d'etat* in the middle of a war shows something, too, of their organizational ability. I am firmly convinced, Max, that they are the people to rebuild their country, make it a part of greater Europe again, and so are the President and most of the leaders of Congress. Oh, there'll be purges, but not blood purges, and with mutual economic support from the rest of Europe, there's little chance the economy will fail."

"I am certainly happy for the world, sir," Tag said. "But how do I fit into all this? I'm a tanker, sir, not an economist."

"Well, Max," Kettle said, "not all of Ivan's troubles are economic."

"China, sir?"

"China, Mongolia—that whole can of worms—yep. We thought the Chinese were eyeballing Japan—and they may have been—but when things fell apart for the Soviets here, the Chinese began nibbling at the other end. Oh, they had the usual pretexts, propaganda about reuniting Mongolia, coming to the aid of freedom-loving guerrillas, and so on, but that was all smoke and mirrors. Nobody bought it. Now, intelligence expects a big push in the spring, one that may not stop at the Mongolian border.

"We can't let that happen, Max, not if we expect to successfully prop up the Svetlovists in Moscow. That's one of the reasons we have allowed them to keep one entire army fully mobilized—the First Guards Tank Army."

"First Guards!" Tag blurted, nearly upsetting his egg-shell coffee cup. "Those were the bastards that nuked us. Hell, General, I just spent the whole damn war fighting that bunch—at your orders. Why them?"

Ross Kettle held up his pipe and spread three fingers for Tag to calm himself. "I thought you might have that reaction, Max," he said. "But in a nutshell, it's like this: first, it's an army built around armor, and armor will be what's needed in Mongolia; second, with the exception of its general staff and regimental political officers, most of its officer corps are professionals who earned their positions, and most of that corps is intact; and finally, it's somewhat of an act of atonement."

General Kettle smiled with satisfaction.

"Sir," Tag said, "if the general will forgive me, I don't think I like where all this is going."

Kettle grinned evilly at Tag. "It gets better, Max," he said. "While we—the Allies, that is—are perfectly willing for the Russians to maintain a standing army in Asia to defend the eastern flank, we still want a presence there ourselves, even if only a token one. Mongolia, as you know, is still an independent republic. So, we are acting on the request of a sovereign government to send additional troops and matériel to support our new allies, the Russians."

"And we're it—the additional troops, I mean?"

"Not exactly, Max. You're more like the matériel. There are two tank brigades, one French and one British, already being assembled to provide most of our manpower. But while the late hostilities were still in high gear, our people in R and D were coming up with some ultralight armor that never made it to the field, a little item called the Terrapin, designed as an antitank weapon, actually, and I think it has tremendous potential for the terrain and the tanks and the tactics you'll see the Chinese using in Mongolia.

"What I want you to do is this, Max: you'll be paired with the commander of the First Guards antitank reconnaissance regiment and be in charge of training indigenous troops in the use of the Terrapins. You will, of course, still have the XM-F4, but for security reasons we have removed some of your equipment, particularly the satellite links."

"And I get to keep my crew—all my crew?"

"Lieutenant Ruther will continue as your driver and my intelligence officer," General Kettle said, reading between the lines of Tag's question. "Like you and Sergeants Jefferson and Tutti, she has been permanently attached to NATO command."

Registering the fact that he had not this time been given the option to volunteer, Tag said, "So, where are these box turtles or whatever that I'm supposed to be the expert on?"

"We have two of them here, out at the tank range, along with your XM-F4. The rest are on their way by train to Berlin, which is where you will catch up with them in four days. You'll be meeting your Russian counterpart there, as well, then travel by train to Ulan Bator."

"You make it sound awfully simple, sir," said Tag.

"Piece of cake," said Ross Kettle.

2

The Terrapin was every inch as homely as its namesake and many times as tough. But slow it was not. No larger than a three-quarter-ton personnel carrier, the Terrapin was wheeled armor, with four large, studded honeycomb tires mounted on four-wheel independent struts that could be extended for crawling over rough terrain or telescoped back under the armored fenders for whipping along on its turbine at speeds up to 110 kph. Its mono-polar "slick skin" armor, identical to that on Tag's XM-F4, the No Slack Too, had been roughly fashioned into a body with a high rear platform, where a low, flat turret mounted a stubby 105mm multi-gun, and a lower forward deck, with a 37mm Phalanx cupola set off-center, beside the driver's hatch. Racks on top of the turret could accommodate either anti-air or antitank missiles. It called for a crew of two but could be operated by a single man from the driver's seat.

"Ugly little suckers, ain't they?" Ham Jefferson said. "No Japanese fit-and-finish work here."

"Yeah," Tag said, circling one of the Terrapins and running his hand over the stealth-polymer paint, "they did a quick and dirty to get these out."

Tag and the crew had just completed a four-hour crash course in a mock-up of the Terrapin's crew positions with a range officer at the NATO tank park, and now they were giving the actual machines the once-over, while mechanics and technicians put the final touches on them before a shakedown run on the range.

The No Slack Too was, as Kettle had promised, also at the range, and Tag, Giesla, Ham, and Fruits had all shared a flood of mixed emotions on seeing it again. Many of the worst hits it had taken—marked by gouges, creases, and shallow puddles—were still visible beneath the fresh coat of stealth paint, like the puckered irregularities that mark an old veteran's wounds. But all its electronic systems— with the exception of the satellite visual links, which had been removed—had been revamped, all its weapon systems checked and recalibrated, and it sported the newest tungsten/polymer track cleats. To a tanker's eyes, the No Slack Too was a work of art.

Compared to it, the Terrapins, which the techs and mechanics now declared ready to roll, were bathroom graffiti—crude, graceless, but not without effect.

"Okay," Tag said, "Giesla, you and Fruits take the number three Terp, and Ham and I'll take the four. We'll run the road along the gunnery range to shake down the turbines, cut back across the impact area to test the suspension, then back to the firing line for some target practice. Any questions?"

"Yeah," Fruits Tutti said. "Any bets on who gets back first? I got a case of beer says da Gies is gonna wipe youse guys' lights."

"Oh, my, my," Ham said, shaking his head. "Captain, I do believe we have a man who wants to wager."

"It is not a wager," said Giesla. "It is theft. We will have German beer, thank you."

Tag cocked an eye at her and said, "We'll see about that. You punters saddle up."

Tag and Giesla slid through the forward hatches and into the drivers' seats, with Ham and Fruits in the gunners' chairs behind and slightly above the drivers' positions. It was cramped in there and gave Tag the feeling that he was more wearing the machine than riding in it. He settled a CVC on his head and adjusted the volume on the radio-intercom. He strapped in and took a minute to review the control console before he hit the ignition and gave the command: "Spin 'em up."

The Terrapin turbines sang to life. Without another word, Tag dropped his transmission in gear and, spinning smoke and loose asphalt from all four tires, shot from the tank park, leaving Giesla and Fruits standing in their shadow.

"Woof, woof," Ham hooted. "The old turtle has got some legs, Boss."

The transmission bumped into a higher gear, the speedometer passing 80 kph, and Tag said, "Yeah. Let's stretch 'em."

Still accelerating, he partially extended the suspension, elevating the Terrapin a foot and widening its wheel base just enough to maintain good handling. Tag could feel a slight wind drag tugging against the Terrapin now, but the speed readout continued blinking higher numbers. He backed off to 90 kph and activated all his defensive warning systems. Immediately, the radar/heat sensors posted the approach of Giesla and Fruits in the other Terrapin.

Tag waited until Giesla's vehicle was within a hundred meters of him, then he hit the throttle again. In seconds, the two Terrapins were running abreast, making more than 100 kph down the macadam access road along the range. Eight-thousand meters later, the road turned to dirt, and Tag made a skidding right-hand turn into the the cratered impact area of the range, jacking up the suspension as he did and stiffening the air-torsion shocks to absorb the terrain.

Giesla spun her Terrapin 180 degrees and shot off at an angle to Tag's route. Working the suspension like a piston assist, she sent the squatty weapons platform sailing over hummocks and the lips of craters, reading the crazy contours of the impact zone as she steadily accelerated.

"Oh, oh," Fruits whined from the gunner's chair, "please don't do dis to me, Gies."

Coming out of the drainage ditch that cut through the middle of the range, Giesla nearly collided with Tag, both Terrapins shying aside and going up on two wheels. Giesla caught the point of balance and brought herself down on all four. Tag was not so lucky.

Hauling on his steering yoke, Tag struck a rut, and the Terrapin, top-heavy with its struts extended, flipped sideways, rolled, bounced upright, and rocked to rest, its turbine stalled. He spun the engine back to life and slammed the throttle wide open, but it was no use. He watched Giesla juking her machine among the shelled-out truck bodies and carcasses of tanks that were used for targets. There was no catching her now.

When Tag pulled into the firing positions at the head of the range, Giesla was leaning casually against her Terrapin, and Fruits was sitting on the lip of the turret hatch buffing his nails on the front of his jumpsuit.

Ham Jefferson popped through his turret hatch, looking a cross between angry and scared, and shouted to Fruits, "Hey, sucker, double or nothing on the targets."

"Yaaa," Fruits sneered. "Make dat *good* German beer."

The range officer in the tower nearby put an end to the squabbling by ordering the two Terrapins into positions fifty meters apart. Three hundred meters downrange sat a row of truck and tank hulls, strung across the range as though in convoy. When the range officer ordered them to commence fire, Ham and Fruits started from either end, racing for the ninth target in the middle. It was no contest. Ham Jefferson was still the best gunner Tag had met. Ham got the ninth target, as well as Fruits's eighth.

When the range officer called a cease-fire, Ham keyed the radio in his CVC and said to Fruits, "Not bad shooting, for a pervert city boy."

"Ah, bugger your shoes," came Tutti's reply.

Tag's voice cut through the chatter. "Okay, sweethearts, I'm glad to see you're all in form. Let's get these machines back over to the park and let the mechanics see what we shook loose. We'll all get another chance at 'em tomorrow."

Over the next three days, Tag and his crew learned everything they could about the Terrapins on the range and, under the tutelage of Colonel Barlow, Kettle's staff liaison, studied every work Kettle had written on what he called the "dragoon strategy," developing specific tactics compatible with what they were learning about the Terrapins.

On the fourth day, a pair of Hercules transports moved them, the Terrapins, and the No Slack Too to Berlin, where they landed at midmorning in spitting sleet and snow and were met by their former project officer for the development of the XM-series tanks, Colonel Roger "Satin Ass" Menefee, all five-feet-four-muscle-bound inches of him. Colonel Menefee was wearing a yellow 7th Cavalry scarf tucked beneath the collar of his greatcoat.

"Surprised to see me, Captain?" Menefee asked as he returned Tag's salute.

"Well, yes, sir, I am," Tag said. "General Kettle didn't give me any idea you'd be here."

"I told him if you knew, you might not volunteer."

"No fear, Colonel," Tag said. "He didn't tell me I was volunteering, either. But why are you here? If you don't mind my asking, sir."

"You're a lucky man, Captain Max Tag," said Menefee with a grin. "I'm your CO again."

Fruits Tutti, who was hopping from foot to foot and flapping his arms nearby to keep warm, emitted an audible moan.

Menefee eyed him sharply, but Tag said, "What's the deal, Colonel? I mean, I thought I was working with a Russian colonel."

"Yes," Menefee said, "an old friend of yours, I believe.

Don't worry, Max. You're still in charge of what you do in the field, but the general wanted someone of equal rank to be in titular command."

For the first time, Tag noticed that Menefee's silver oak leaves had been replaced with eagles. "Oh," he said, "congratulations, sir."

Menefee nodded and went on: "Have your men get their gear. I'll drop them at the transient barracks and take you and Lieutenant Ruther to the BOQ. You and I have a meeting with your friend Colonel Yeshev at eleven-thirty hours."

Tag's estimation of Menefee went up a notch when he saw that the colonel had finagled a Mercedes staff car, which he drove himself. He'd also arranged adjacent quarters for Tag and Giesla at the BOQ and had the manners not to leer about it. Tag thought the war might have civilized the man.

Tag had just enough time to change into a dress uniform before Menefee was back to get him at 1115, and the two rode in the olive-drab Mercedes past rows of white barracks regular as tombstones, out the gate of the base, and onto the loop road, heading south of the city, toward the suburb of Kopenick. Menefee took the first exit into Kopenick, made a series of turns through narrow streets between anonymous warehouses and what looked like abandoned factories, then stopped at one of these and, with a remote control clipped to the visor of the car, opened the heavy metal loading bay that faced the street.

"What's all this about, sir?" asked Tag.

"Let's just say, Max, that we've found it easier to get some things done away from that cluster fuck they call the Military Assistance Group. The MAGgots were about to drive me nuts with committees on how to cut your orders, how they should read—should it be 'all reasonable force' or 'all necessary force.' Fuck it. We—you and I and Yeshev— will work it out. We've got forty-eight hours here and five days on the train, so let's don't waste any time reminiscing about all the good times we've had together. Okay?"

Menefee stopped the car and shut the door behind them.

"I," Tag said, affecting a sniffy diplomatic drawl, "hold no briefs concerning the late unpleasantness between our two countries."

"Damn straight, you don't," said Menefee. "Come on."

Tag followed the squatty colonel through a steel door, down a cold, dim corridor that smelled of old machine grease, and into a large, well-lit office, divided into cubicles by movable partitions. Just inside the door to the room was a sergeant sitting behind a desk in a U.S. Army uniform. He rose and saluted and said, "Colonel Yeshev is in the operations room waiting for you, sir."

Menefee led Tag through the warren of partitions and into another, smaller room, where a large contour table had been set up next to a wall covered with maps and acetate overlays, and in one corner was a sitting area, with a sofa, several easy chairs, tables, and lamps arranged on a rectangle of oriental carpet. Two men in Russian uniforms rose from sofa. Tag recognized one of them.

"Colonel Yeshev," said Tag, stepping forward and offering a salute.

Feyodr Oblanovich Yeshev waved off Tag's salute and came toward him with his hand extended. "Captain Tag," he said, "Butcher Boy, it is a pleasure to see you again . . . under these circumstances." The big-shouldered Russian, perhaps ten years older than Tag, had improved his English since his surrender to Tag in the Swabian Jura the previous fall, but he smiled in a way that made Tag think it was not easy for him.

Tag shook his hand and said, "Yes, Colonel, I agree. Alpha Fox, weren't you? Colonel Menefee tells me that we have a lot to talk about in a very few days."

"Yes," said Yeshev, "we do." He made a half turn and put his hand on the shoulder of the tall, balding, bespectacled major standing behind him. "This," he said, "is Major Pavel

Minski, my operations officer and formerly a professor of tactics at our war college."

Tag leaned forward and shook Minski's hand.

"I have been reading—or rereading, I should say—your General Kettle's books," said Minski with a distinctly British clip to his Russian accent. "I am anxious to work with you, Captain."

"Well," said Menefee, "let's get to it then."

The four men gathered around the contour table, and Minski unclipped a telescoping metal pointer from his pocket. Extending it with a theatrical flourish, he turned to the map on the wall. Cross-referencing his lecture between the map and the table, Minski launched into an hour of detailed background information on the history, politics, terrain, and climate of Mongolia, with asides on how these things pertained to the current situation. By the time they broke for lunch at 1300 hours, Tag's head was abuzz with facts.

Along with his beet soup, roast beef, boiled vegetables, and black bread, Tag tried to digest Minski's briefing. The history was fascinating, and the politics Byzantine, but what mattered most to Tag were the conditions he'd be fighting and training his men in. The steppes he could imagine from the high plains of Montana, but the Gobi was something else. It was a high, cold, rocky desert, blown with heavy sand and dust as fine as talc. Men and camels, whole caravans, had choked and been buried by the frigid storms that sometimes swept the Gobi in overwhelming waves of sand and dust. And Tag knew that those same storms could choke a turbine engine faster than they could a camel.

If Minski was right, he would have to launch some sort of training as soon as possible, even if it was nearly February, because the Chinese armored divisions massing in Outer Mongolia would want to start any push before spring thaw, before the mud got deep and the river beds ran high. The grazing country he could prepare for, but the threat from across the Gobi to the southwest was a puzzler. Still, if the Chinese could penetrate it, so could he. Somehow.

The next day and a half that he spent listening to Minski, asking questions, and getting to know Yeshev were like two months of war college. As things now stood, there would be regular line units of Russian and Mongol armor in place to take the main body of the expected Chinese advance from the south and southeast; it would be the responsibility of Yeshev's skeleton regiment and the Mongols Tag was to train in the use of the Terrapins to stop any enveloping elements moving in out of the Gobi or off the flank of the main attack. The remains of Yeshev's regiment, already shipped to Mongolia, included a half-dozen of the advanced T-80B tanks, fifty or so T-80s, ten old T-64Bs, and some two dozen of the beefed-up 2S9s, as well as an equal number of assorted wheeled armor—BMPs and BRMs in antitank configurations. Of the lot, only the T-80Bs had impressed Tag in combat, but the Chinese wouldn't be in XM-F4 tanks, either. Their armor was mostly T-72s—the older export models that the Soviet Union once supplied— and domestic knockoffs of T-64Bs. Tag liked the idea of using the Terrapins and 2S9s against them.

Most of the meetings were intense, all business, but through them, and over coffee and meals, Tag came to a guarded respect for Yeshev. The man was a professional, tough and smart, but seemed still to be suffering some sort of inhibition in his relations with Tag and Menefee. The situation was ambiguous, Yeshev's future murky, but Tag could only hope things worked themselves out. For now, there was too much to do.

The weather grew colder, and the rain had changed to snow by the morning of their departure. Their Trans-Siberian Express was five boxcars containing the Terrapins, five more of ordnance and supplies, a flatcar for the No Slack Too, two cars of troops—one NATO, one Russian—for security, and a dining car between two sleep-

er coaches, all hauled by three Russian diesel locomotives.

Ham and Fruits had to bunk with the other enlisted swine
from Yeshev's headquarters in one of the two sleepers, but
the one behind the dining car was reserved for the five
officers—Tag, Giesla, Menefee, Yeshev, and Minski—and
had been gutted of one of its compartments to make a com-
bination lounge and briefing room, complete with a small
contour table and map stand.

Tag dropped his duffel in the middle of the lounge and
took it in with a thin whistle.

"Now this is what I call officers' quarters," he said.

The interior of the car was out of some other era. It
was paneled in oiled teak with mahogany trim and brass
fixtures. The doors to the compartments were made of
carved oak, as were the seats in the lounge, which were
furnished with tapestry cushions and bolsters to match the
heavy drapes drooping around the windows. There were two
bathrooms—one with a bidet, much to Giesla's delight and
to the discomfort of Menefee and the Russians—each with
a tiled shower and piles of thick, soft towels. Each of the
compartments had a bed that folded against the wall and two
cushioned, cane-bottom seats facing across a small built-in
table beneath an antique light fixture converted to use an
electric bulb.

By tacit agreement, Tag and Giesla took two adjacent
compartments at one end of the car, with the bathrooms
and lounge between them and the others. Once they had all
unpacked, Yeshev ordered a tray of sweetbreads and a huge,
steaming samovar of tea from the dining car. Tag drew
himself hot tea in a glass he held in a silver filigree caddy
and, following Yeshev's and Minski's example, sweetened
it with a dollop of raspberry jam.

The snow thickened as the train rolled out of Berlin,
crossed the Oder, and forged through the featureless plains
of northern Poland. Warm inside their car, around the hissing

samovar, the uneasy allies felt the snow settle like a blanket around them, wrapping them together. They sipped tea and nibbled rolls in silence for many minutes, before Minski broke the ice with some small talk to Giesla. Soon, they were all talking casually, which soon led to discussion of armor, and then into serious matters, with Minski and Tag taking turns to present their assessments of the developing situation in Mongolia and various strategic and tactical considerations.

They worked throughout the day and part of the evening, turned in early, and awoke the next morning to a landscape of dazzling white. Just after breakfast, they stopped for fuel in a small city inside Russia, and Tag sent word for Fruits and Ham to join him and Giesla on the flatcar of the No Slack Too.

The morning air was still and brittle with cold, the sky washed blue, and all around, even in the usually sooty environs of the train yard, the shapes of the things of the world were softened by the deep sifting of snow. Most of it had been blown off the XM-F4, but the canvas gun covers were stiff as iron, and the restraint chains had that dull glint of a frozen pump handle, so inviting to the tongues of children.

"Hey, you yo-yos," Tag called to Ham and Fruits, who were banging on a frozen hatch, Fruits just beginning to tug a mitten off with his teeth, "don't you touch any metal barehanded."

"Whadda ya mean, Cap?" Fruits mumbled through his mitten.

"I mean," Tag said, "that you'd rather be pissed on than pissed off, when your tongue is froze to the pump handle. Got it?"

Fruits slipped the mitten back on, and in a few minutes they were all inside the No Slack Too.

"Spin 'em up, Gies," Tag said, and Giesla touched the ignition.

It took a few more turns of the starter than usual, but the

turbines finally caught. In a few more minutes, the crew compartment was warm enough for the crew to come out of their parkas, and Tag began a preliminary check of the systems. Satisfied that he had continuity in the electronics, he gave the order for each position to check out its primary-use systems. Ham rotated the turret and took sightings through all his target-acquisition devices; Fruits worked the loading carousel and twisted the Phalanx cupola on manual hydraulics; Giesla revved the turbines, checking their vital signs; and Tag monitored everything on the command console.

When it was time to pull out, Tag said to Menefee, who was standing on the rear platform of their sleeping coach, just ahead of the flatcar, "Colonel, I want to keep the crew in the tank for a while, see how it does with the cold blowing through it."

Menefee waved and went quickly back inside.

Even before the train left the yard, word had gone out to the renegade brigade of hard-line communists hiding in the forests beyond the town. The word was that this was a commando unit come to root them out.

It was an eerie sensation, to be moving in a stationary tank, but Tag and his crew were happy as kids with their favorite toy, chattering over the intercom and abusing one another's ancestors. Just past the last suburb, about ten kilometers outside town, the train entered a stretch of thick forest that crowded against the railroad right of way. The snow was deeper on the tracks here, and the locomotives labored behind the plow blade on the front. Fruits Tutti was toying with the Phalanx thermal sensors, whose software he had modified, trying to pick up a heat blip from a deer or, in his imagination, a bear, when the cold striations of the trees were suddenly winking with heat images in a bend of the tracks just ahead.

"Hey, Captain Max," he said, "lookit dis. I think I got a herd of moose of somethin'."

Tag glanced at his own screen, did a double take, and said, "Double-check that, Fruits. Looks to me like they're multiplying."

Sure enough, Fruits could detect more and more of the blips, and none of them were running away.

"Max," said Giesla, "I do not like this."

"She's right, Bossman," Ham said. "This deal stinks of ambush."

"I reckon you'd know, Hambone," said Tag. "Lock and load. Fruits, stand by the Phalanx."

As the carousel hummed and the barrels of the Phalanx ratcheted rounds into their chambers, Tag and Giesla jacked belts of 7.62mm ammunition into the breeches of their coaxial machine guns.

Tag wanted to alert the rest of the train, but they were coming up on the bend too fast for him to get to the other cars in time. Should he fire a burst to alert them? Would that give away his element of surprise against the ambush? What if it wasn't an ambush? What if it was a bunch of woodcutters? Nobody said anything about hostiles out here. Would the recoil of the 120mm knock them off the flatcar?

As these and other thoughts ran through Tag's mind at a gallop, the train bent into the curve, opening up the No Slack Too's fields of fire to the front and left, where the sensors had picked up the blips. Scanning the tree line through his optical scope, Tag saw the first two contrails from RPGs diverging from the forest and felt their impacts on the boxcars behind him at the same moment he shouted, "Fire!"

The recoil of the 120mm shook the entire flatcar, but the restraint chains held, and the wheels stayed on the track. The trip-hammer trill of the 37mm Phalanx ran through the slick-skin armor, and Tag shook to his shoulders from the recoil of his coax machine gun, as the crew poured ordnance into the renegades' positions. Flaming stumps marked the impact of the 120mm HE round, and the depleted-uranium slugs from the Phalanx exploded tree trunks at two thousand rounds a minute, while Tag and Giesla strafed the length of the ambush.

Suddenly, they were all pitched forward, as an RPG struck the lead locomotive's carriage, blasting loose a wheel and sending the suspension grinding into the rails, as the second engine tried to jackknife against the first.

"Beehive in the tube," Tag ordered, and Fruits seated an antipersonnel canister in the breech.

By now the security troops in the cars at the front and rear had joined the fight and were falling out to counterassault the ambush. Small arms fire was thick, and another RPG struck the No Slack Too, blossoming harmlessly against its armor.

"Fire," Tag ordered, and the thousands of darts in the beehive round scoured the edge of the woods.

A second RPG struck the disabled lead locomotive, sending an orange fireball boiling from its midsection. Under cover of the inky smoke that poured from the fire, the engineers rushed to disconnect the burning engine.

The sleeper coach in front of him prevented Tag from laying the main tube on the far end of the ambush, but he had an angle with the Phalanx, and ordered Fruits to hose down the positions still firing RPGs at the train. He directed Ham's 120mm on the near flank, to cover the advance of the security troops now moving across the right of way and into the woods, and kept up a steady rhythm of short bursts from his own 7.62mm machine gun.

In ten minutes, it was over. More than thirty of the ambushers lay dead, the rest scattered in the forest.

The engineers backed the rest of the train away from the burning engine and called for a crane and crew from the next station to come and clear the track.

Tag and the crew unbuttoned and climbed out onto the flatcar. Two of the boxcars containing the Terrapins had taken RPG hits, and the cornice work on the sleeper coach had been shattered by small arms fire. The No Slack Too had lost a patch of polymer finish.

"Fruits, Ham," he said, "go check out the Terps. We'll check on Menefee and the others."

"I thought these muthafuckers were our pals," Ham said.

"Yeah, Ham, I know," said Tag. "It's a helluva world where you got to fight your way to the war."

3

Because of the ambush and the delay, they passed through Moscow at night, without a layover, and by the next day were in sight of the Urals. Three days beyond them, across the white, featureless expanses of Siberia, the train turned south and entered Mongolia, arriving at last at Ulan Bator, a city of nearly a half-million people and only one building more than five stories tall, that the dilapidated joint-venture hotel that the Peninsula Group had misguidedly erected in cooperation with the Mongol government in the mid-nineties, where Yeshev took Tag, Menefee, and the crew.

The atrium-with-rooms-attached architecture gave Tag and Giesla a laugh, looking as it did so much like the dozens of hotels they had stayed in on their tour of America. Here, however, the fountain in the lobby was dry, the planters on the balconies empty, and the glass elevators stalled between floors.

No officers or civilian officials had met them, only two Volga sedans and two jeeps full of soldiers for security to the hotel, which had its own resident platoon.

"These people act like they're already on red alert," Ham Jefferson said.

"The whole country's like that," said Menefee. "They've been expecting the balloon to go up for more than six months now."

"So, how close are we to da action, sir?" Fruits asked.

"Our bivouac's about a day's travel from here, Sergeant," said Menefee. "And we leave in the morning, so enjoy your stay at the Mongol Hilton."

That night, Yeshev took everyone to Ulan Bator's only Russian-owned restaurant, where despite the cold and the grimy surroundings of the concrete building, they enjoyed caviar on toast and drank strong, lemony vodka before demolishing a pork roast, one tureen of dumplings and another of some unidentifiable Mongol greens, bowls of borscht with yogurt, and perhaps three dozen jam tortes, along with a samovar of black Russian tea. As the plates were being cleared, Yeshev swirled a balloon of brandy over the candle on the table and proposed a toast:

"To success," he said, "and, I hope, to friendship."

When they had drunk, Tag responded.

"To our mission," he said, "and to the fury that is armor."

"To a new world order," said Menefee.

Everyone looked askance at Menefee, but they drank six toasts in all (Fruits would not offer one) and drove back to the hotel fuzzy with travel and drink. Tag and Giesla fell giggling into the same bed, and it was morning before they knew whose.

The train trip the next day took four hours, traveling southwest from the city. They arrived at a military compound, where Russian troops unloaded the Terrapins and transferred the supplies into trucks, getting an earful from the men in the security detail about the RPG hits on the boxcars. Tag left Giesla to oversee the crew and the unloading of the No Slack Too, while he met with the Russian tankers from Yeshev's regiment who would be ferrying the Terps to the bivouac, some forty kilometers away. After giving them a short course on driving the Terrapin, Tag turned that job over to Giesla as well and went on to Menefee's office, which would be Tag's headquarters in Mongolia.

Sharp grains of sleet flew in the wind beneath a sheet of

clouds that hung like a failed ceiling over the rolling waste of the Gobi stretching beyond the concrete buildings and barbed wire perimeter of the compound. The bivouac, Tag thought, is going to be a real dandy.

Yeshev and Minski were already in Menefee's office when Tag arrived, and the muscular little colonel got right down to business.

"Max," Menefee said, "I wanted to go over the ground rules with you one more time, with Colonel Yeshev and Major Minski here to hear it. Your primary responsibility is to train the Mongol troops in the operation and tactical use of the Terrapins. Secondly, you will act as tactical adviser to Colonel Yeshev, and give Major Minski any assistance he requests. You will consider yourself part of the field-headquarters staff and will take your orders from me, either directly or through Colonel Yeshev, who has total discretion in the field. Understood?"

"Yes, sir."

"Any questions?"

"Are the Terrapins my command?" Tag asked.

"They are your responsibility," Menefee said. "This sector is under Colonel Yeshev's command. You're here to train, Max, not to fight. Those are Kettle's orders."

Tag said, "Yessir," and shut up.

Within an hour, the convoy was assembled, trucks in front, and the No Slack Too leading a column of twenty Terrapins, one of which had Yeshev at the controls and a reluctant Major Minski in the turret.

"Alpha Fox," Tag radioed through his CVC, "this is Butcher Boy. How do you like your ride? Over."

"This is Alpha Fox," Yeshev replied. "A very nimble turtle, I think it is. And not too much room. Over."

Tag smiled at the joke. "Butcher Boy out," he said.

It was a landscape as bleak as the moon that Tag saw through his optical scope, whole vistas of strewn boulders, hills barer than the mountains of Oman and desiccated by cold, with here or there, on some lonesome rise, a cairn of stones the Mongols call an *ao bao*, serving as a place of religious devotion, a navigation mark on the otherwise featureless terrain, and a rendezvous for lovers. Ignorant of this, Tag saw them as aiming stakes.

It wasn't hard for Tag to see what troops were in the bivouac. Among the tanks around most of the perimeter were heavy Russian winter tents, quilted with insulation and pitched over reinforced wooden frames. But in one sector stood a cluster of yurts, the round felt-covered shelters with conical roofs that are the traditional homes of the nomad Mongols. Tethered near them was a string of forty or fifty small, shaggy Mongol ponies.

Yeshev invited Ham and Fruits to the officers' mess, where he introduced them to the crew of his personal T-80B: Yuri Kasmarov, the driver; Dmitri Tsarpov, the gunner; and Zig Gogol, the assistant gunner and field mechanic. As Ham and Fruits were leaving for the enlisted men's mess, two Mongols entered the tent, one in uniform and the other in bizarre civilian dress that included baggy Mongol herdsman's breeches and high leather boots, a pink cummerbund, a two-tone green designer sweater, a heavy dun-colored parka, and a ballcap with the logo of the Yokohama Giants.

"Ah," said Yeshev, "this is Captain Tambur, whose men you will be training, and the fashion model is your translator. Call him Titz, Captain Tag; you could not pronounce his real name."

Tag and Giesla shook hands with the Mongols, and Captain Tambur said, "Very glad to make you," to them both, and Titz said, "Hi, what do you know? Much?"

"Titz," said Yeshev, "is supposed to speak Mongol, English, Russian, Chinese, and Japanese, but if his other languages are like his Russian, you may need a translator for his translations."

"I bet we'll manage, sir," said Tag. "I'll want me and my

crew billeted with Captain Tambur and his men, if that's okay, Colonel."

Yeshev nodded. "Titz and Captain Tambur can show you where after we eat."

Their conversation over the roasted mutton in the officers' mess was cursory. Tag learned that Tambur had sixty men under him, most of them either green recruits or ninety-day wonders from the Mongol Army's officer school. More than half had arrived at the bivouac on horseback, and maybe a dozen had ever driven anything with wheels and a motor. Among those were six experienced mechanics, a couple of truck drivers, a conscripted cabby, and a heavy-equipment operator. Tambur himself was officially a tanker, but he had spent the past two years as a staff officer in Ulan Bator. Still, Tag liked him. Tambur was sturdily built and moved with physical confidence. His face was serious and intelligent, at times as impassive as that of a Plains Indian, and at others bright with humor.

Titz was another matter. The civilian translator suffered from some form of logorrhea, making it almost impossible for him to shut up once he began one of his weird, slangy riffs.

"Too cool, Slim," Titz said to Giesla, who had just offered some pleasantry about Tambur's non-drivers not having any bad habits to unlearn. "*Tabla rasa*, that's where these cats are at. Technological blank slates everyone. Machines aren't Mongol macho, you know? But they are bad tough hombres. It's like this time, must have been the thirteenth century. . . ."

And Tag and Giesla and the Russians sat agape for more than fifteen minutes while Titz recounted the loric battle of an obscure khan, using language mostly excavated from a motley of textbooks and Hollywood movies of the sixties.

Tag knew that it was going to be another strange assignment.

Tambur had a yurt made ready, and being a Mongol, he

thought nothing of Tag and Giesla staying together—or of Ham and Fruits sharing the yurt with them. The floor of the yurt was covered with a thick, loosely woven carpet of blue and white wool, worn threadbare in patches. Sheepskins and blankets thick as rugs were heaped on four low rawhide-laced cots, and in the center of the yurt sat a small coal stove with an eight-quart tea kettle steaming on top. A stack of gear was piled by each cot, and in two of them lay Ham Jefferson and Fruits Tutti, each with a one-liter bottle of beer in his hand.

"Now isn't this cozy," Tag said as he stood on his knees in the the weak light from an electric lantern inside the yurt.

"Better believe it's your best bet for now, Captain," Titz said behind him.

Tag grunted, and Ham said, "Welcome to the house party, y'all. That'll be officers' country over there to your right. You'll find washbasins, towels, and tea making in that wardrobe trunk."

"Delightful," Giesla said, sounding as though she meant it.

"Good night," said Titz, ducking back out the door flap.

"Sneak well," said Captain Tambur, letting the flap fall.

Giesla put loose tea from a tin in a covered ceramic cup and filled it from the kettle on the stove. Tag mollified himself with a beer Fruits offered him and filled them in on what sort of troops they would be training, along with his impressions of Tambur and Titz.

Ham and Fruits, in turn, talked about Yuri, Dmitri, and Zig, the crew of Yeshev's personal tank, all of whom spoke some English and were very strack troopers, despite Dmitri's obsession with women and Zig's fighting opinion about Russian rock music's superiority to that of the West.

"Yeah," Fruits said, "dat Zig is one political animal. I just wisht he coulda met dat Sergeant N. Sain."

"Oh, yeah," Tag echoed. "The Dark Disciple of retro-rock. That would have been a real cultural collision, all right. But we've got one of our own coming in the morning, I'll bet. Let's hit it, sweethearts. And no peeking while your lieutenant gets into bed."

The sound of one of the Mongol troopers stoking the coal stove woke Tag early the next morning. He struggled from beneath the weight of his bedding and put his head out. The temperature inside the yurt was frigid. In the time it took for Tag to find the switch on the lantern and look at his watch— it was 0430—his ears had begun to ache with the cold. He pulled the jumpsuit on the floor beside him into bed and warmed it under the covers before putting it on.

Dressed at last in boots, down pants, and parka, Tag was already returning from the latrine—a truly chilling experience—when another Mongol trooper arrived with their breakfast of oatmeal, goat cheese, honey, and bread, all in a single covered bucket of the sort people used to use as chamber pots. Tag didn't see things getting any better.

After morning formation, at 0630, just as the sun was rising, Tag left Giesla and the men to get acquainted and start work on the Terrapins, while he went with Tambur and Titz to the operations tent, to start working out a training schedule with Major Minski. The more the light rose and the better he could see the desolate face of the Gobi fringe, the more glum Tag became. At least the wind had dropped and there was no sleet. But the scattering lid of clouds still hung low and it was colder than the day before, hovering at five degrees Fahrenheit.

Given the personnel they had to work with, getting everyone trained was going to be a problem, Tag thought, and he spent most of the day in Minski's S-3 tent trying to hammer out a plan, uneasy because he seemed to be the only one worried about the weather. Two hours before dark, he called it a day at the desk and took Tambur to look over the Terrapins and take his first spin in one.

The Mongol mechanics and Russian technicians had done

the routine preparation and preventative maintenance on the Terps, and Fruits and Ham had begun checking out the weapons and electronics systems. Giesla, who had just driven one of the Terrapins around the Mongol compound of the perimeter, to the cheering delight of the Mongol soldiers, pulled up beside Tag, Tambur, and Titz and leaned out of the driver's hatch.

"This one is warm, if you want to take it," she said.

"Give Captain Tambur here the ground course, will you, Gies? I'll have a look at how things are going and be back in a few minutes."

It wasn't hard for him to find Ham and Fruits, once he got through the curious crowd of Mongols who had gathered around the Terrapin they were working on.

"How's it going?" Tag asked through the open driver's hatch.

"Nothin' too flaky," Fruits said, tapping a digital readout with his finger. "But we been havin' fits to keep dese Mongol guys outta them."

"Hell, lock the ignitions and the systems and let 'em," Tag said. "They're going to be driving these buggers in a week."

"Shit, Boss," Ham said from the turret, "these dudes are most of 'em still working on gee and haw. They think the fuel goes down the barrel."

"Well," Tag said, "you're a trainer, Jefferson, so train 'em. Show 'em anything you can."

"And I thought boxing was a lousy business," Ham muttered.

"What's that?" Tag asked.

"He said, 'Yes, sir,' " Fruits answered.

Giesla had Tambur negotiating figure-eights with the Terrapin by the time Tag got back to them, and he took a few more minutes to go over the weapons systems before putting the Mongol captain in the turret and taking the controls himself. He steered them through a zigzag gap in the perimeter wire and out into the frozen desert.

With Tambur looking over his shoulder from the gunner's seat, Tag demonstrated some of the Terrapin's capabilities, its speed and suspension and handling, then offered the controls to Tambur.

"With pressure," said the Mongol.

Tambur took it easy at first, following Tag's instructions with some uncertainty, but gradually he gained confidence, began to get the feel of the machine, and pushed the tachometer up the numbers. Running with the struts half-extended, Tambur took them up to 100 kph, gripping the yoke hard in both hands but moving the Terp deftly through the scatter of rock and boulders. He steered to the top of a rise on the right, where a well-used track curved up to an even higher rise and the nearest *ao bao*.

Tambur stalled the Terrapin when he tried to stop by the pile of stones, but did not seem to mind, for he was out of the hatch in seconds, beaming at the sky, the hood of his parka thrown back. Tag stood in the turret hatch and watched as Tambur collected an armful of fist-size stones from the ground and began tossing them up toward the top of the mesa-shaped cairn while shouting out a chant that Tag thought too loud to be a prayer.

Tambur walked back to the Terrapin and said to Tag, "God knows Terrorpin. God give Mongol curveage. Make you braid, too."

Tag climbed out and picked up three stones. "Okay?" he said to Tambur.

Tambur nodded vigorously. "Okay. Okay," he said, making an underhanded throwing motion.

Tag lofted the stones, one at a time, as though he were tossing his hat on a shelf, and all three of them landed and stuck on the top of the pile.

"Oh, oh," Tambur said. "God give you big curveage."

By the time they were back at the bivouac, night was falling, and Tag was more optimistic about his Mongol tankers than he had yet been. If they all showed the knack Tambur had, Tag would make armored cavalry out of them in thirty days, as bad a bunch as ever laid an ambush. He had done it once with a bunch of semiliterate Omanis and Bedouins, and he sensed some definite parallels of character between those sons of Allah and these descendants of the khans.

The weather held—cold but snowless—for several days, and Tag began to see some real progress in the training, especially after Yuri, Dmitri, and Zig became a part of it, for the Russians were quick studies on the Terrapins. There were plenty of language problems—Tambur and a few others spoke some broken English, and most spoke a little Chinese, as did Yuri and Giesla, and everyone ended up relying on Titz's improvised translations—but a few commands in English and Chinese fell into common use, and Tag was beginning to feel that he was establishing a bond with this group of half-disciplined, semicivilized recruits, and he was continually surprised by their instincts for tactics.

"You should not be," Colonel Yeshev told him one evening over tea and vodka in the officers' mess. "These men have been in training as cavalry for centuries. I sometimes think it is still in their blood: one morning the entire race will wake up and know it is time to pillage Europe once again. They are herdsmen and hunters. I have seen a Mongol stalk within bowshot of a gazelle across open country—no cover, you understand. And wait until you see one of their horse races or polo games."

"Polo?" Tag said.

"Mmmm," murmured Yeshev, sipping his tea. "They play it with a sheep's head, although an enemy's is traditional, I have heard."

The more Tag learned about the Mongols, the easier he found it to believe Yeshev. And the more he learned, the more they reminded him, in looks and in spirit, of American

Indians. Their discipline was casual but distinct. There was not a lot of saluting by the men or much shouting by the officers, but everything got done. No man ever missed a formation or failed to show up for a work detail. And despite the cacophony of languages, the Mongols were moving through Tag's training schedule the way prodigies zip through a textbook. Within ten days, he had them ready to start learning the guns.

Returning early one afternoon with ten of the Terrapins from a live-fire exercise, trying to beat a storm moving down on the bivouac from Lake Baykal in Siberia, Tag took the notion to give the Mongols a pop quiz in tactics.

"Giesla," he said over the intercom of the No Slack Too, "when I give you the word, I want you to wheel left and give us about three-quarter throttle. Go about a kilometer, then haul back right and look for a two-tiered rise with an *ao bao* on top."

"What's up, Bossman?" Ham asked.

"We're just going to play a little fox and hounds, Hambone. See what our people have learned. Hit it, Gies."

As Giesla spun rocks from the treads of the No Slack Too, Tag keyed the TacNet and croaked out a line he had learned from a Mongol folk song, a love lyric that, loosely translated, meant "meet me at the *ao bao*."

Giesla was a splendid driver. She was fast and deft but projected none of the recklessness that had been the earmark of the XM-F4's original driver, Wheels Latta, who had died in the war in Europe. Instead, she seemed analytical, and a close observer felt he could almost read her thoughts. She drove like the rally driver she had once been, calculating every obstacle at lightning speed, and following those calculations with precise maneuvers that lost no time or effort.

The country was open but unfamiliar to Giesla and littered with the ubiquitous rocks and boulders. So, even with the No Slack Too riding high on its own extended suspension, she had to sacrifice some speed to safety, slowing as she topped the rolls of the earth and skirting wide around sandy depressions that might swallow the tank like an ant lion's trap.

To add something special to the impromptu test, Tag had released a billow of obscuring smoke from the No Slack Too's defensive systems, and neither he nor any other member of his crew caught sight of the Mongols in the Terrapins once the chase was on.

When Giesla saw the *ao bao* on the rise, she opened the throttles full-bore and whipped the No Slack Too up the switchback and brought it to a rocking halt at the foot of the cairn. Tag threw back his hatch, winced at the biting cold, and said over the intercom, "Just act casual when our guys get here. Remember that we're trying to train 'em, not show 'em up."

"Guess again, Boss," Ham Jefferson said. "Take a look-see at your nine o'clock."

Tag looked to his left, and there, barely peeping over the crest of the rise, were the muzzles of three 105mm guns. He looked back to his right, and there were four more just creeping into view from behind the rubble of stones.

"Well, kiss my U.S. Army ass," Tag muttered.

Captain Tambur appeared over the rise and waved at Tag. "Gotcha. Gotcha," he shouted, using a phrase he had picked up from Titz. "You sender? You our prismers now, Captain Tag."

Tag held up his hands and grinned. "Yeah, yeah," he said. "We surrender."

Tambur motioned for the Terrapins to close on the tank and walked toward it himself, pleased and cocky.

"How the hell did you people get here?" Tag asked.

Twisting his mouth to contain a grin, Tambur said, "We opay order, meet you at *ao bao*. Is okay?"

"Is better than that," Tag said. "Let's get ourselves back to camp before this storm breaks."

"You know where way?" Tambur asked slyly.

"I'll follow you," Tag said.

Tag had seen his share of blizzards while growing up on the high plains of Montana, but nothing he had experienced could compare to the Siberian storm that swept down on them that night. It hit the bivouac like a fist—wind, snow, sleet, and sand that had no prelude, just a sudden and total engulfment, like a *tsunami* sweeping over a coral atoll. Tag and the crew were sitting on the ends of their cots, wrapped in sheepskins and huddled around the small warmth of the coal stove in the yurt, when Major Minski threw back the flap and scuttled inside amid a swirl of snow that settled on the rug without melting.

"Good evening," Minski said genially, shaking the snow from his fur hat. "I have just received some information that I thought might interest you, Captain Tag."

Tag stood and turned his cot to give Minski a place near the stove. "Sit down," he said. "Fruits, fix the major a cup of tea, will you?"

While he waited for the tea, Minski said, "Are you enjoying this little bit of Siberian winter?"

Tag shivered beneath his sheepskin. "Major," he said, "it feels like there's nothing between here and the North Pole except a picket fence."

Minski laughed softly. "Yes," he replied, "we have a similar saying in Russian, except that we add that the fence is down." He took the tea from Fruits and handed a manila envelope to Giesla. "I believe you read Russian, Lieutenant Ruther," he said. "You may want to look at this while I speak."

Giesla opened the envelope, took out a sheet of onion-skin, and read it as Minski talked.

"Earlier today," he said, "while you were in the field, we began receiving reports from the line units to the east that a reconnaissance patrol had encountered a Chinese unit fifty kilometers inside the border. Subsequent reports stated that there had been contact and some casualties. Just a few minutes ago, I received the report that Lieutenant Ruther is now reading. According to it, the infantry clash was much larger than we were first led to believe, involving perhaps a battalion of Chinese troops.

"A mechanized column was sent in relief of the reconnaissance patrol, along with gunships for support, but the storm came on them before they could locate the Chinese."

"Did they find the patrol?" Tag asked.

"What was left of it," Minski said, "but I do not know what intelligence they brought back."

"Well," Tag said, "that is interesting. Still, I don't see why it brought you out on a night like this just to tell us."

"This storm will be past by morning," said Minski, waving a hand at the roof of the yurt, "but the Chinese may, as they have done before, try to move troops and tanks into new positions under its cover. Once it stops, they will also. There will be too much fresh snow, and it would be easy to see their tracks from the air or even satellites. Colonel Yeshev has been called on to inspect the units in that sector, to help them prepare antitank defenses, and he has asked you to join him, you and your crew and tank."

"Aw, peachy fuckin' keen," Fruits whined. "We get to go dashin' through the snow."

Tag gave his loader a look but said to Minski, "But surely they wouldn't attack. I mean, it's the dead of winter, and we could get another storm anytime, from what Titz tells me."

Minski shrugged and pushed his glasses up on his nose. "History, Captain Tag," he said. "Remember your Korean War, the Yalu River and the Chosin Reservoir. The Chinese are often daring strategists, if poor tacticians. They have only a slight edge in numbers now, and are much inferior in equipment, so they may very well want to make the weather their ally."

Tag nodded and sucked on his cheek. "And I don't suppose they've changed their strategy that much in fifty years."

"Captain Tag," Minski said, setting aside his tea and pulling out his mittens, "they haven't changed that strategy since the thirteenth century, when they learned it from the Mongol khan Ghenghis."

4

Despite a quilted tent thrown over the No Slack Too during the night, Ham and Fruits had to use propane torches to thaw the hatches the next morning, working in iron-hard cold, the temperature creeping up to twenty below by 0700. By the time the turbines were started and the physical and electronic systems on-line, Yeshev was ready in his T-80B, and the two tanks rolled out of the zigzag tank gate in the perimeter, their belly pans skimming the foot of fresh powder on the ground.

Warm inside the No Slack Too, with a cup of bitter instant coffee to sip and little else to do, Tag patched his VDT into the external video camera and watched the surreal landscape roll past. The blanket of snow was even and complete, blurring the few distinctions of topography that the land offered and turning the occasional *ao bao* into a soft serac. Once, they passed a line of concrete power poles, the wires sagging beneath impossibly high, narrow accumulations of snow, and once Tag caught a distant glimpse of three woolly Bactrian camels high-stepping through the drifts. Otherwise, the scenery was unbroken until they reached the flank of the division that Yeshev had come to advise.

The division was a hodgepodge of Mongol infantry and Russian armor from the First Guards, with British Harrier jump jets and attack helicopters for air support. Most of the aircraft, however, were grounded as a result of last night's

47

storm, their parts frozen and fuel jelled in the bladders.

At the command center for this flank of the line, Yeshev dismounted and approached the No Slack Too. Tag came up through his hatch and stood there slapping his hands together as Yeshev walked up.

"Captain Tag," Yeshev said, his words falling as stars of frost, "while I am looking at the dispositions on the map, I would like you to conduct a physical inspection of the emplacements. Be back here in one hour to brief me, then I will also inspect them, and we can start back before twelve-hundred hours."

"How far down the line do I need to go?" Tag asked.

"Until you reach the French brigade, about ten kilometers."

"We're on the way," said Tag.

From what Tag could see without getting out and inspecting the positions on foot, the First Guards had done a good job of digging in. Each tank along the line had at least two alternative fighting positions, and they had made good use of the subtle differences in elevation to command deep, overlapping fields of fire. The infantry positions were less to his liking, but he had already learned that the Mongols had a powerful predisposition against defensive tactics that he was not likely to change in one morning inspection. He was bothered also by the number of T-72 tanks that had been used to shore up the First Guards' depleted ranks. As far as Tag was concerned, the T-72 was little better than highly mobile field artillery, although still a match for anything the Chinese could put in the field.

"Jeez," said Fruits Tutti, scanning the mixed collection of armor on his own VDT, "they got a buncha fuckin' museum pieces out there. Didja see them T-54s?"

"Those are the Mongols' contribution, Fruits," said Giesla over the intercom. "Look at the markings."

"I can read that," said Ham Jefferson. "They all say 'helicopter bait.' "

"Well," said Tag, "we don't have much to worry about on that score. 'Chinese air power' is another one of those famous oxymorons, right up there with business ethics and jumbo shrimp."

"Yeah," said Fruits, "but don't forget 'holy war' and 'military intelligence.' "

Tag was back at the command center within his allotted hour and found Yeshev already set to go.

"How did you find the positions, Captain Tag?" asked Yeshev.

"Just looked and there they were," said Tag. But, seeing the puzzled look on the Russian's face, he added, "The armor emplacements were good, Colonel. I can't say the same for the Mongol infantry, though. And I hope to God we don't have to actually use any of the Mongol tanks."

"Both of us," Yeshev replied. "I think it is not necessary for me to inspect the positions again, if you believe there are no serious problems. After looking at the maps, however, I want us to make a circle forward, into the area where the fighting took place yesterday. I am now more concerned about the open country between here and our bivouac than about the possible threat from the desert. Do you feel like a little drive?"

"My calendar is open," said Tag.

Yeshev smiled. "Good," he said. "Follow me."

"All systems up," Tag said. He punched in the code for the LandNav system, and at once a topographic image sprang onto his VDT, with the No Slack Too as a green blip moving across it. He recalled the general location of the action from the maps in Minski's operations tent, but the low contours of the terrain gave him no clue about what Yeshev might hope to find there. Tag would have given six months' pay for a satellite link.

The two tanks moved through the snow-softened landscape utterly alone. No bird or animal stirred on the frozen undulations of the Mongolian steppe, and even the sounds of the tanks' engines were muted by the deep mantle of powder that their belly pans slipped over, leaving leveled berms of ice between the tread ruts. Moving from the image on his VDT to the eyepieces of his optical scope, Tag was struck by the eerieness of it all and could imagine how absurdly small the two pieces of main battle armor would appear to an eagle. He also noticed how, in the lee of certain formations of the rolling plain, snow dunes formed overhangs and deep cavities. He looked for something like these on the VDT image and saw what Yeshev must have already known, that there was a ring of high ground to the southwest of the battle site, forming a shelter like the breakwater to a bay, like a blizzard fence along a Montana highway.

"Gies," he said, touching a light stylus to the VDT screen, "mark this grid; it looks like our objective. Ham, you look it over, too. Fruits, sabot in the main tube. Arm the Phalanx and the War Clubs."

The loading carousel hummed; the Gatling barrels of the Phalanx spun and locked; and Tag confirmed the systems from his console.

"Alpha Fox, Alpha Fox," Tag radioed to Yeshev, "this is Butcher Boy. Over."

"This is Alpha Fox. Over."

"Alpha Fox, I have gone to full ready. Please confirm objective as follows: from Vodka," Tag said, using the code name for the line positions they had just left, "down one five, left two zero. Over."

Tag heard Yeshev's grunt of approval before the Russian answered, "Confirmed, Butcher Boy. Confirmed full ready. Hamstring. Do you copy? Over."

"Roger. Hamstring. I copy. Butcher Boy out."

Giesla looked at Tag and mouthed the word "hamstring" silently.

Tag grinned and nodded. Hamstring was one of Kettle's terms, the one he used to describe the tactics for two tanks engaging a larger but outgunned enemy, likening it to the way a pair of wolves can pull down a half-ton elk, one worrying the nose and the other crippling its hindquarters. Obviously, Yeshev thought this something more than a Sunday drive himself.

Tag felt his adrenaline begin to rise, clearing his head and warming him from the inside. With the growing anticipation of contact, he also felt how exposed they were, two black masses against the unbroken white of the land, without concealment or cover. Checking their location and projecting their route, Tag had a hunch that Yeshev already had this excursion planned: he was taking them on a path that stayed off any silhouetting rises and out of the deep-drifted beds of the dry spring-rivers, always keeping at least two rolls of the land between themselves and their objective, working around it from the north.

This and hamstring, too. Tag was impressed.

Confident now in Yeshev's tactic, Tag let his personal alert status drop a notch and turned his attention to his console. One amber readout light showed him that the Phalanx active radar was not up but on standby, keyed to the passive radar detectors. He fiddled with the focus on the LandNav display, squinted at the amber light, and punched the Phalanx radar up to red.

Almost before his finger was off the button, the muted klaxon of the air alarm began its frantic honking. Tag slapped for the kill switch above his head and cued the radar image for his VDT.

"Got a lock," Fruits Tutti said, his voice dry with excitement. "Trackin' right at three-four-one-four. Range: twelve thousand meters. Speed—shit, he's loafin'—speed: four hunnert kph."

"Confirmed," Tag said.

"What do we got, Boss?" Ham asked.

"It's big, it's low, it's slow, and it ain't ours," Tag said. He shut down the radar and spoke to Yeshev.

"Alpha Fox, this is Butcher Boy. I have low-flying unknown aircraft on radar at azimuth three-four-one-five. Can you confirm? Over."

Yeshev said, "Wait, Butcher Boy," and then there was a long silence before he came up again.

"Butcher Boy, this is Alpha Fox. Aircraft confirmed. Disengage active radar. Do you copy? Over."

"Roger, Alpha Fox. Already done."

"Butcher Boy, could you identify the target? Over."

"Negative, Alpha Fox. Judging its size and speed, though, I would say a transport."

"Roger, Butcher Boy. We are going directly in, alternating rushes the final three kilometers."

Without a sign-off, Yeshev heeled his T-80B to the left and accelerated up the rise of the ground, churning rooster tails of a skier's dream from beneath his treads.

"Swing to his right rear, Gies," said Tag, "and lay off about two hundred meters, whatever the traffic will allow."

Giesla hiked the No Slack Too a few centimeters higher on its air-torsion suspension and eased open the throats of the turbines. There was enough ice and hardpack beneath the powder for easy running as long as she kept them out of the drifts, but there were boulders that lay like submerged snags in a muddy stream, and Giesla could not afford to take their bottom out on one of them. She read the masked land as deftly as a blind man skims a page of Braille, finding cover from the horizon in every transit of a knoll and keeping Yeshev in glimpse at each one.

Fruits Tutti scanned the low overcast through the optical link at the Phalanx auxiliary console.

Tag swept the same sky with the snout of the audio-directional sensor, hoping to pick out the hum of an aircraft seven miles away and glancing anxiously at the amber glow from the radar switch.

"Holy shit," Fruits blurted. "Captain Max, key on me. Dere's shit fallin' outta da sky. No shit."

Tag locked onto Fruits's sighting and twisted up the magnification on his commander's scope. Shit falling from the sky: big boxes beneath clusters of parachutes. And right where they were going.

He contacted Yeshev, who confirmed the drop, then said to Tag, "Butcher Boy, can your missiles hit that aircraft?"

Tag had a passing moment's smug satisfaction. The modified Tree Toads that the T-80B carried were hot rockets, but had a range of six thousand meters, tops. The War Clubs on the No Slack Too were rated out to ten thousand, but Tag knew from experience that that was really pushing the envelope.

"That will depend on my radar and the direction of his turn," Tag said. "I need to get on him now."

"Take your place, Butcher Boy. We will hold position. Alpha Fox out."

"I want the first high place you can give me, Gies," said Tag.

Giesla quartered up the steep side of a rise to their right and brought the XM-F4 to rest astraddle of the crest.

Tag tripped the radar to red and had a blip in seconds. The transport was banking back in his direction and gaining no altitude, obviously attempting to stay below the radar horizon of the ground stations behind the Mongol lines. Tag armed the War Clubs and locked them on the radar return. When the arc of the blip on his screen began to bend away from them again, at about nine thousand meters' distance, he released a pair of the missiles.

"Two away," Tag said, as a pair of the needle-nose War Clubs sizzled from their clamshell farings.

In the moments before the missiles found the Chinese transport above the low overcast, things began happening very fast.

"Butcher Boy," Yeshev's voice suddenly broke over the radio, "this is Alpha Fox. Fast-approaching aircraft at two eight hundred."

Before Tag could respond, the air-alarm klaxon bellowed, and the active radar locked on a second blip, whose size and speed said it was a fighter.

"Reverse. Air-evasive action," Tag said.

Giesla goosed the turbines, and the XM-F4 slithered back off the crown of the hill, narrowly escaping a hit from a missile that lifted a geyser of ice and snow just feet from where they had been sitting. In the middle of all this, Tag never saw the burning rain of wreckage that fell from the clouds, the remains of the Chinese transport. What he did see was a red-orange fireball cartwheeling out of the cloud almost directly above him, with just enough of one wing still protruding from the falling inferno to identify it as a plane. It hammered in beyond the next rise, throwing up a dark mushroom of smoke, but immediately there was another fast-moving blip coming onto his screen. Tag released a third War Club, which was swallowed by the overcast. On his screen, however, Tag saw his weapon find its mark, as a second Chinese copy of a MiG-31 shattered in midair, its radar image becoming a shower of electronic confetti.

"Butcher Boy, this is Alpha Fox. Report. Over."

"Roger, Alpha Fox," Tag replied. "Okay here. Nice shooting. I owe you one. Over."

"Roger, Butcher Boy. Now we run. Alpha Fox out."

Tag nodded to Giesla and said, "Go."

The No Slack Too fishtailed up a broad draw between two hills, crossed a saddle, and was back within sight of Yeshev's tank in less than a minute. In another minute the two were racing nearly abreast across the frozen, rolling plain.

At three kilometers from their objective, Tag and Yeshev began the leapfrog tactic, one covering the other as they alternated their advance, taking a route that would lead them to the western edge of the arc of hills, near where airdrop had taken place.

Covering the last kilometer before they had to break into

the open, Tag responded again to the air-alarm klaxon, as two more low, slow blips flickered on his screen, these moving to the west, just out of War Club range.

"Alpha Fox, this is Butcher Boy," he radioed to Yeshev. "I have two more bad guys moving west at three eight hundred."

"Confirmed, Butcher Boy. Proceed."

"Roger. Out."

"Captain, I got movement at ten o'clock," Fruits Tutti said. The customized tuning he had done of the Phalanx closed-loop radar software at last was paying off, for at ranges up to one thousand meters, Fruits could sort out human forms from the ground clutter.

"Track 'em with the Phalanx, Fruits," said Tag. "Giesla, pour on the coal. I don't think we're gonna surprise anybody here now."

Tag checked the feed on his 7.62mm coaxial machine gun and keyed the TacNet.

"Alpha Fox, this is Butcher Boy. We have troops on foot at two niner eight zero. Distance: eight hundred meters. You copy? Over."

"Alpha Fox copy. Follow me."

"Roger. Butcher Boy out."

Yeshev pushed his massive T-80B to the red line. With the No Slack Too speeding at his right quarter-flank, he broke from the folds of hills and into the open country beyond. As he—and, later, Tag—had suspected, the ring of high ground had left a series of blown-snow overhangs in the lee, and the heat and radar sensors on both tanks came immediately to life.

"Targets," Ham Jefferson sang out.

"Butcher Boy," Yeshev said over the radio, "take the nose. I will be the stretch."

"Roger," Tag replied. "Gunner's choice," he said to Ham. "Fruits, back him up on the Phalanx. Giesla, let's head for the barn."

The first two shots from the Chinese tanks concealed in the snow dunes were not even close, both whistling wide and long. But at less than one thousand meters, Ham was not likely to miss much.

He touched off his first sabot in the middle of Giesla's turn and struck the ChiCom T-72 clone just beneath the turret. The secondary explosion from the penetrator core of his round shuddered inside the crew compartment, filling it with melted shrapnel and searing heat. Ham got his second shot off to the rear, under the cover of withering bursts of depleted-uranium slugs from the Phalanx. The second sabot tore through the side of another T-72 and erupted as a jet of burning fuel from the air intakes on the rear deck.

Yeshev had sprinted back north, and Giesla was taking an angle that would soon have the No Slack Too out of the flat country and back into the relative cover of the lumpy hills, where Yeshev should be headed, positioning himself to pick off any pursuit.

Baffled by the tanks' tactics and Giesla's daring slalom, the Chinese gunners did little more than break the monotony of the landscape with their salvos of fire. Four of them broke from their positions to give chase.

"Let 'em stay close enough not to give up, Gies," said Tag. "I'd like to give our Russian buddies something to shoot."

Giesla bent their path up the back of a rise, exposed their profile on the horizon for one moment, then was off again as the Chinese steered toward her.

"Butcher Boy, this is Alpha Fox. I have you covered."

"Roger, Alpha Fox. Giesla, take the next fighting position, there, behind the low shoulder of that hill."

Giesla spun the No Slack Too behind the rise that Tag had indicated and crept up the slope, until the turret was peeking over the crest.

"Targets," Ham said.

"I'm with you, Hambone," Tag said. "Mark one."

"Mark one," Ham responded, locking his IR laser scope on the lead Chinese tank, now less than a thousand meters away.

Tag waited until he could see all four of the pursuing tanks before giving Ham the order to fire.

The sabot flew from the 120mm and collapsed the glacis of the T-72. The metal puckered around the entry hole made by the penetrator core, and the explosion inside seemed to lift the tank momentarily, before it settled to a smoking halt, still jolted from inside by rupturing fire extinguishers and overheated cylinders of halon gas.

The remaining Chinese broke their formation, attempting to come on-line to assault Tag's position. As they did, the drag tank suddenly went up in a roar of flames spreading over it from the hit it had taken in its rear grille from Yeshev's T-80B.

"Target," Ham called.

"Shoot," Tag ordered.

"Shot."

A third T-72 went down on its chassis, its left track and fender ripped away by the 120mm sabot.

"Splash," Tag said. "Fruits, wipe up that mess with the Phalanx."

The heavy roll of recoil from the big chain gun throbbed through the No Slack Too.

"Target," Ham said again.

"Shoot."

Ham's round and the one from Yeshev's tank reached the surviving T-72 almost simultaneously, creating a blast that lifted the turret off the body and hailed pieces of hatch and armor plate for a hundred meters around.

Tag spotted Yeshev's tank coming from its position, speeding through the smoking remains of the Chinese formation and racing past the No Slack Too.

"Follow that guy," Tag said to Giesla, and she swapped

ends with the XM-F4, digging a semicircle with one track
as she turned on the slope.

Tag checked his radar screen again and found that the two
blips he had seen earlier were returning in the direction from
which they came. They were already moving out of the War
Clubs' effective range, so he decided to give it a pass, but
with a few quick key strokes he calculated the speed and
direction of the aircraft to give himself a good idea of where
they had been. Yeshev was headed right for the spot.

Even through the deep snow, the two tanks covered the ten
kilometers that they had to travel in less than fifteen minutes.
The two hundred Chinese paratroopers were still trying to
group up in the open when Tag and Yeshev brought their
machines into positions overlooking the drop zone.

Yeshev said over the radio, "Take them."

"Load HE," Tag said. "Forward at a trot."

Giesla ground forward over the crusting snow.

"Hambone," said Tag, "shoot till you poop."

The 120mm roared, echoed by Yeshev's gun, while Tag
and Giesla opened up with their coax machine guns and
Fruits alternately fed the 120mm and let off microsecond
bursts from the 37mm Phalanx.

With the two tanks moving on them fast from different quarters, the Chinese never had a chance. Caught by
surprise and in the open, they panicked. Many threw themselves to the ground and huddled in terror, others made a
show of returning small arms fire, and only a few had the
discipline or presence of mind to unlimber their antitank
rockets, managing not to hit anything but to draw lethal
attention to themselves from Tutti's Phalanx.

It was a massacre. The two hundred winter operations
troops, specially trained for months in Tibet for this infiltration, had not come prepared for a hot DZ. Circling and
shooting, the American tank and the Russian one closed
the noose tighter with each lap, leaving at last four blood-
spattered acres of corpses stiffening on the snow. In the

middle of it all, where some of the Chinese had rallied and tried to make a stand, it looked from Tag's distance like a steaming heap of intestines spilled from a gutted elk, the blood freezing before it could turn brown.

Yeshev brought his T-80B up beside the No Slack Too and called for Tag to put his head out.

"What's up?" Tag shouted from his open hatch.

"We must search for physical intelligence," Yeshev yelled, "and very quickly."

Tag had been thinking about the time himself, and about how far from their original route they had strayed, but he knew that Yeshev was right about needing to sift the bodies for documents and maps.

Tag left Ham and Fruits to tend the tank, while he and Giesla, along with Yeshev and his crewman Zig Gogol, spread out to search for what they could find. It wasn't made any easier by the fact that the Chinese wore no rank insignia, but map cases and dispatch pouches could still be found, and some of the dead, the older ones, especially, wore better boots and gloves than others, and Giesla rightly guessed that she might find documents on them that would be useful. In fifteen minutes, they had gathered what they could and were glad to be back in the warmth of the tanks and again moving rapidly for their own bivouac.

They arrived back at the camp in the last shadows of the day and found Major Minski in a professorial tizzy, distracted with worry over them and the sketchy reports they had radioed in from the field. Did they not know that there were now scattered reports of Chinese infiltration units coming in from civilians having recently fled from the more remote settlements of the interior? Did they know of the latest storm developing in the north?

Yeshev slapped his own shoulders and stepped closer to the stove in the operations tent.

"Pavel Ivanovich," he said, adding the old-fashioned familiarity of Minski's patronymic, "we are here. You may stop being concerned for us. Please, prepare me a briefing on the dispatches. Lieutenant Ruther, Captain Tambur, and the translator are going over the material we took from the paratroops. They should know something by the time you have completed the briefing."

"Yes, yes," Minski said. "Of course. The samovar is hot, Comrade Colonel." He went to the message center, where three men were monitoring radios, took up a folder of coded sheets, carried it to a pulpit desk nearby, and bent over the sheets in concentration.

Yeshev drew tea for himself and Tag, and they sat down on folding stools next to the stove.

"While we await the facts," said Yeshev, "what do you make of what we saw today, Captain?"

Tag sipped his tea, then said, "It worries the shit out of me. Did you ever study the disaster of the Little Big Horn, Custer's Last Stand?"

"Oh, yes."

"Well, I don't exactly feel like the Indians right now. I think Charlie ChiCom probably knows where we are and how many we are. He just doesn't know who we are. And paratroopers in the winter—this is not just for drill, Colonel. My hunch is that they're looking for a way to wiggle through the crack between us and the western flank, throw enough shit in there that we won't be any kind of factor in cutting them off. Use the strength of their numbers, same as always. Anything they pull out in the Gobi itself is just a ploy. What was it Mao said about making a noise in the west so you can attack in the east?"

Yeshev nodded and smiled glumly. "A very colorful analysis," he said. "So, let us hope for bad weather and a little time to see what we may do."

Tag raised his cup. "Think snow," he said.

5

The first thing Tag was aware of when he awoke was that there was no sound of wind, no shifting and tugging on the yurt frame. It was as though the silence had a weight. Dragging his sheepskin bedding across his shoulders, he knee-walked to the small stove, shook the clinkers through the grate, and tossed two double handfuls of coal on the glowing remains of the fire. He wondered why the Mongol who usually fed the stove was late and felt a little cranky about it. He was hungry, too, hungry enough that the usual breakfast fare of barley gruel and yogurt sounded good to him. So where was it? Tag grumbled to himself until the coal caught and began to knock the chill off the yurt, then he bundled himself in his parka and insulated trousers, ready to go in search of food.

The stiff flaps over the door of the yurt were frozen shut, and Tag took a tin plate to chip them apart, hacking with its edge until he could separate the leather inside flap from the felt one on the outside.

"Hey, what's happening?" Ham said sleepily from his cot. "You digging a tunnel, Boss?"

Tag butted the flap with his shoulder. "May have to, Hambone," he said. "I think we've got a drift over the door."

Now Tag could hear the sounds of Mongol voices and

laughter, then the sounds of digging, and in a minute or two Titz lifted the outer flap and stuck his head through a round opening in the solid sheet of snow covering the door.

"Cowabunga, dudes," he said, all smiles. "You sleepy-heads getting up today, or what? You'll miss the party, if you don't get hopping."

"Party," Fruits whined from beneath his covers. "What kinda freakin' *party*? The freakin' deep-freeze follies, that's yere fuggin' party."

Giesla suddenly leaped from her cot and whipped the pile of bedding off Fruits.

"Up, up, Francisco," she said. "It is the winter wonder-land."

A pile of snow fell through the door, with Titz on top and still chattering away. Sunlight spilled through the opening, and Tag caught a whiff of wood smoke and roasting meat.

Fruits snatched at the covers and said, "Gimme dat," while Ham groaned and rolled tighter in his sheepskins.

"Up, up and at 'em," Tag shouted over the din. "I can smell breakfast cooking."

"That's right," Titz said. "Today we feast to celebrate your victory over the Hans. Food, sports, a real deal, man. Then, more snow tonight."

"Okay. Okay," said Tag. "We can't all call time-out at once. Giesla, take charge of these maniacs. Get them fed and put 'em to some PM on the No Slack Too."

"You want to be alone for a while, Boss?" Ham asked.

"No. I think I'll have a power breakfast with Freddie Yeshev, though. I want to see what G-2 has put together." He turned to Titz. "You're for real about that snow?"

"Real as heart attack," Titz said.

Tag went on all fours out the door and up the bank of snow. He stood and blinked in the blinding white of the day, fumbling with his mittened hands to pull the polarized goggles down off his forehead. The snow that had drifted over the door to his yurt, which was facing away from the wind, was nothing to the mogul formed by the yurt itself, complete with a windblown overhang, like a miniature of those in which the Chinese had hidden their armor. Every yurt in the Mongol camp was turned into a smooth tumulus of snow, with one or more of the tough, shaggy ponies tethered by the door. The Terrapins beneath their makeshift covers of Russian tents formed bizarre snow sculptures, all planes and creases and protrusions. Nearby, at the center of the sprawl of yurts, the Mongols had built a large fire; and over it were four whole sheep turning on spits. The men around the fire were not in uniform but wore the bright, barbaric costumes that remained civilian dress for many Mongols. One of them came running up to Tag, carrying two steaming buckets and wearing tin teacups with dangling lids like rings on both his hands. The man sat the buckets in the snow, which began to melt around them, then at once to refreeze, took four cups off his fingers, and asked Tag something in Mongolian.

"He wants to know if four is all you need," Titz said from the door of the yurt. "I'll take one too."

Tag held up five fingers, took the cups, and tossed four of them over the low drift and into the door. One of the covered buckets—he still thought of them as slop jars—contained a gallon or so of strong, smoky tea made with milk and sweetened with fruit preserves. Tag dipped himself a cupful and handed the buckets one at a time to Titz.

"Party hearty," Tag said.

The Russian winter shelters hadn't stood up beneath the snow as well as the yurts. Many of the quilted tents were swaybacked with snow, and more than one of the wooden frames had snapped and let a wall slump beneath a leaning drift. With the crews not yet turned out to clear the tanks and shovel paths between the tents, the place had an air of abandonment, like a ghost town's, only here there was no tumbleweed, and it was snow, not sand, that blew between the tents. The fresh powder squeaked beneath the lug soles of Tag's expedition boots. He stopped and sipped from the lidded mug, holding it between his mittens the way a seal would.

He had seen these bright, still days that fall between two blizzards in Montana, and recalled the old-timers saying that the second was always worse. Today, however, he did not care. He had duties to attend to, of course, but there was a sense that this day was somehow exempt, special. Did the Mongols sense that as well? Was the fighting yesterday only an excuse for the festivities today? There would be no fighting today, perhaps not even an air strike on the Chinese staging area, and the next storm, even if no worse, would dump enough snow to slow everything for several days. Tag was anxious to get his work done and check out the roasted mutton.

Inside Yeshev's headquarters tent, Tag was introduced to a young captain named Dzhukov, the stop-gap intelligence officer for Yeshev's depleted regiment.

"It seems that our after-action report has multiplied to haunt us," Yeshev said. "Captain Dzhukov was up all night, and Major Minski and I have been going over the information for two hours now."

He waved one hand at the pile of message sheets on his field desk.

"The professor will be back soon," Yeshev continued, "and he can begin the briefing. Captain Dzhukov does not speak English very well, I am afraid, especially when he is tired."

He spoke to Dzhukov in Russian. Dzhukov laughed and said, "*Da, da,*" before he nodded to Tag and left.

Tag accepted Yeshev's offer of breakfast and ate powdered eggs, canned sausage, and hard bread until Major Minski returned.

"Well," said the operations officer, peering over his fogged spectacles as he shed his parka, "your paratroops have caused quite an interest at command, Captain. And your colonel, Menefee, wanted me to ask you if you had stopped taking prisoners."

Tag glanced at Yeshev, who shrugged and said, "Tell Colonel Menefee that I will order Captain Tag to send him the next one."

Minski wiped the lenses of his glasses and grinned at Tag with bright, shortsighted eyes. "Let us get some tea, Captain," he said. "This will take little time."

The gist of Minski's remarks was that, while the intelligence about the strength of the Chinese armor in the area and the presence of large numbers of winter operations troops was significant, there were too few troops on the main lines of defense to risk redeployment. A flanking maneuver in any strength by the Chinese was unlikely, although some sort of flanking effort was certainly probable, most likely as a diversion. In sum, the orders remained essentially unchanged. Only the alert status was to be changed, from condition two to condition one, just short of open war.

"Have they given us any higher priority for air support?" Tag asked.

"Colonel Menefee seems to believe he can get aerial photos sent to you by radio-facsimile," said Minski, "but they would be twenty-four hours old, perhaps more. But no tactical support, no."

"Peachy," Tag mumbled. He bit a plug of the tough black bread and chewed mechanically for a long minute. At last, he said, "Colonel, I want to step up the training schedule. I'm convinced those boys can drive the Terrapins, but they need some serious gunnery practice. I've just got a lousy feeling that things are not as rosy as command thinks. And if I am right, the Terrapins are going to have a fat hog to cut. A fat, mean hog."

Yeshev grunted and nodded. "I agree," he said. "By all means. But not today, Captain. The Mongols have a very superstitious attitude about days like this, the days between storms. They call them 'the smile of God.' They think it is an omen that we fought yesterday. But perhaps today you will see some things you should know about these Mongols. Today, I would not be impatient with them."

Tag started to object but caught himself, remembering the infuriating attitudes he had encountered among the Omanis when he first worked with them. It seemed to him that they had a prayer to make or a holy day to observe every time there was some bad duty coming up. Eventually, he had had to accept their religion and their customs and found that they were excellent armor troops, perfectly willing to suspend their beliefs and habits when the chips were down.

"Okay," Tag said. "If it's inevitable, I might as well enjoy it."

Yeshev smiled and rose from his stool. "Good," he said. "Let us see what festivities there are, then."

Yeshev and Tag left Minski to man the headquarters and walked across the bivouac to the Mongol camp. During the hour that Tag had been inside the tent, the crews had started policing the area, sweeping off the tanks and using a BMP with a blade mounted in front to clear paths through the snow. It remained cold and still, but the sun felt good on Tag's face, and by the time they reached the yurts, he was ready to relax and enjoy the day.

The Mongols had been busy, as well. Despite nearly two feet of new snow, they had managed to shovel and scrape and doze (with the aid of two of the Terrapins) a space larger than a soccer field, extending from their compound to the scraggly row of half-buried concertina wire that marked the perimeter of the bivouac. Four goats had been added to the spits over the fire and some makeshift tables set up, on which sat more of the steaming slop jars, a variety of bowls and baskets, and an assortment of wine, liquor, and beer bottles, like those on the back bar of a fancy saloon.

Captain Tambur and Titz met Tag and Yeshev as they entered the center of the camp.

"Creepings, creepings, my friends," said Tambur. "I hope

you to enjoy the festing in your horror. Your victimy was a great horror for all us. Today, we celibate."

Tambur looked very proud of his speech, which Tag had to explain to Yeshev.

"Come on," said Titz. "The wrestling is about ready to begin."

He led them to a place near the fire pit, where the ground had been scraped and strewn with ashes and straw. Inside the circle of men gathered around it, Ham, Fruits, Giesla, and the three men of Yeshev's crew were seated on ammunition boxes, drinking tea and passing a bottle of sweet plum wine. Tag and Yeshev took their places of honor on a pair of leather stools, and Titz explained Mongol wrestling to them.

"It's a piece of cake," the translator said. "No grabbing, no locks, no kicking. Each cat takes hold of the other's vest, and they try to sling each other down, either by tripping or getting the dude off-balance."

"Why the grip on the vest?" Tag asked.

"Oh, man," said Titz, as though having to explain the obvious, "so they won't be whipping out their shivs and juking each other in the ribs."

"Oh," said Tag.

Two Mongols stepped into the circle and took off their long, felt-trimmed fur coats. Each man was wearing high black boots, baggy trousers, and a heavy, double-breasted leather vest festooned with concho-like medallions, bits of cloth and leather ribbons, and small, round silver bells. They took wide stances and circled each other with exaggerated stomping movements, rather like mesomorphic sumo wrestlers, then stepped face to face, each man taking the other's vest by the arm holes and shaking him, snarling and making fierce faces.

A high, wild cheer went up from the crowd, and the match was on.

The two contestants whirled, feinted, and hooked at each

other's legs with their heels, all the while twisting and pulling on the vests, until one of them at last lost his balance and fell, much to the delight of the crowd, which gave another whoop as both wrestlers left the circle. They were replaced by a pair of larger men, the two largest Mongols in the camp, both strapping six-footers with deep chests and thick arms. They repeated the preliminaries, locked up, and contended for almost ten minutes before one of them, attempting a sudden rush forward, lost his footing and went to one knee, ending the match.

Tag was still applauding the wrestlers when two Mongols came up to him, holding one of the wrestling vests open and indicating that they expected him to put it on.

"Titz," he said to the translator, "tell them no, that it's not my game."

"No can do, big kahuna," Titz said. "Heap big insult."

Tag sighed, stood, and began shucking his thick winter gear. He stopped at his long johns, causing a mild titter among the Mongols, and let the two men harness him in the vest. Getting in the spirit of the moment, Tag stepped to the middle of the circle, loosened his arms, flexed, struck a pose, and said loudly, "Okay, suckers, let's get ready to rumble."

There was movement at the back of the crowd, and a few sounds of admiration, as the ring of men parted to admit one of the largest men Tag had ever seen, Mongol or otherwise. Easily topping six-and-a-half feet and weighing something more than bathroom scales could handle, the fellow was obviously a ringer. Tag swallowed hard and searched the faces around him for someone to be mad at. He looked back at his opponent, who had just entered the circle, and saw that the man's features were too small for his face—tiny slits of eyes, a button nose, ridiculously little ears, and a child-size mouth that revealed rows of teeth the size of popcorn kernels when he smiled, as he did now, offering Tag his hand.

"Don't worry, Boss," Ham sang out. "He can run from you, but he's too big to hide."

Tag muttered, "Oh, shit," and went through the stomping ritual, hoping to spot some weakness in the giant, before clapping his hands on the man's vest. It was like taking hold of a tree. And the Mongol's grip on him felt like vises. Maybe, Tag thought, maybe he's clumsy.

Tag jumped and spun and tried to keep his weight low, lashing out with his feet. The simpleton smile never left the Mongol's face. Suddenly, Tag was experiencing flight. The giant grunted and whipped Tag in the air, both feet airborne, then slammed him down on them, gave Tag a moment to recover, and did it again. The third time, the wind went out of Tag and he fell against the man in a clench.

Wild applause went up from the Mongols. Captain Tambur rushed forward and held Tag's head as he poured sweet wine down his throat.

"No one slays so lung with Atla," Tambur said, slapping the gasping Tag on the back. "This is great horror."

Tag coughed and said, at last, "Thank you. You can let someone else have the horror now."

"Yes, yes," said Tambur, "all will be horrored."

Much to Tag's delight, he saw a group of Mongols surrounding Ham and Fruits and Yeshev's crew, holding several of the leather vests for them.

When everyone, save Giesla, had had the horror of wrestling with Atla, Tag showed them Indian arm wrestling, in which two opponents face each other, put their right feet side by side, grip as though to shake hands, then try to unbalance each other. Quickness and balance counted for much more than strength, and Giesla gained a host of admirers by toppling one of the larger wrestlers, who ripped a concho and a cluster of bells from his vest to give to her.

While everyone got back into warm clothes, and fresh

straw was spread over the wrestling area, the Mongols passed the tea and baskets of something hard, white, and sweet that Titz said was dried mare's milk yogurt. Tag was sorry he had asked.

Next came the horse racing. It began with fifty or more riders galloping pell-mell down the length of the clearing, with the obvious losers taking themselves out for the series of elimination sprints that followed. When one man on a yellow, mean-looking pony took two heats, all the rest rushed back onto the field to congratulate him. Someone tossed a frozen sheep's head into the throng, and the polo game was on. Tag could never figure out what the sides were, or whether it was a battle-royal. In fact, he could seldom see the sheep's head or understand what the object was. What was clear to him, however, was that he was in the presence of some of the finest riding he had ever witnessed.

He had known cowboys and rodeo riders who could pull some fancy stunts, but most of them at least had decent saddles and bridles and good horses. The Mongol saddles were no more than a layer of felt tacked over a wooden saddle tree with a ridge down the middle like some instrument of torture. No wonder they all rode standing in the metal stirrups. And the horses themselves—bad-tempered and hardy though they were—were hardly bigger than donkeys. To saddle them, it took three men—one to hold the halter, one to hobble the back legs, and one to tighten the cinch. A man could do it alone only by bulldogging the pony to the ground and trussing it before setting the saddle, and that only if he didn't mind getting bit.

As the polo game was breaking up, men began carrying large straw-stuffed baskets out onto the clearing, and Tambur came up beside Tag and Yeshev, carrying a short recurve bow and a quiver of arrows.

"This Mongo blow," said Tambur. "You like to shoot it?"

"With pressure," Tag said, but Tambur took no notice of his sarcasm and handed him the bow and arrows with a smile.

Tag slipped off his mittens as he walked toward the targets and tried the draw of the bow. It was surprisingly stiff and too short for him, but after a couple of pitiful misses, he put six arrows in a row into one of the baskets from about fifty feet, then passed the bow to Zig Gogol, the assistant gunner from Yeshev's T-80B, who claimed he was half-Tartar and had been born with bows in his blood. Before long, Ham and Fruits and Tsarpov and Kasmarov had joined Gogol in a spirited shooting contest, which was won, as they used to say of the Miss Iran contest, by no one. Then, the Mongols took over.

First from horseback, they came swooping down on the targets, standing in the stirrups and loosing arrows with amazing speed and accuracy, filling the baskets like pincushions. Then, they retrieved the arrows and had a standing shoot-off that wasn't decided until the targets had been moved more than fifty meters away. Surprisingly, one of the finalists was the giant Atla, who, Tag learned from Titz, was considered something of an idiot savant by the Mongols, since he was too large to ride a horse.

By then the meat was done and passed out on metal plates. It was not carved so much as hacked to pieces, intended to be eaten with the hands. Tag found he was ravenous and ate until his chin was slick with rich mutton grease. Then he knocked back a half dozen toasts of plum wine and vodka and felt better than he had ever imagined he could out here on the frozen fringe of the Gobi with a billion Chinese poised to attack from the south.

Soon the music began, and it was more than Tag could stand. One song, played on a two-string fiddle, was much like a bluegrass breakdown, but the singing fell on Tag's ears like fingernails on a blackboard. He caught Giesla's eye and saw she felt the same. She cut her eyes back toward their yurt, and five minutes later they were alone there.

Tag lashed down the inside flap over the door, while Giesla fed the coal stove and opened the dampers wide. In minutes the yurt was stiflingly warm, and they both began coming out of their heavy clothes. Giesla lit a candle and set it on an ammunition box beside her cot.

"I know," she said to Tag, "that we said we would not do this here, but today . . . today does not really exist, does it, Max?"

"Not on any known calendar," he said, sinking to his knees beside the cot. "Today we are outside time, living in the smile of God, as the Mongols say."

Giesla smiled at him and stripped her T-shirt off over her head. She rubbed her breasts and shoulders. "I wish God would smile on me with a shower," she said.

"I've got the next best thing," said Tag. He rattled in the chest for a washbasin, filled it with water from the kettle on the stove, and found a towel and bar of soap in his duffel bag. "Come over here by the stove," he said, "and you can wash my back."

"You are a cavalier, Max," she said, as she wriggled out of her briefs.

They knelt together in the heat of the stove and bathed each other slowly, exchanging soapy kisses and slow caresses until Giesla was panting with anticipation and Tag was suffering the swollen throb of an erection.

He pulled a pile of blankets and sheepskins off a cot and rolled her onto the pallet on the floor. He kissed her face and throat and breasts and belly, ran his tongue along the creases where her legs met her body, then up the moist slit between them, rolling her clitoris gently with his tongue, while Giesla held him by the hair and took her breath in gasps. A shudder passed over her, and she made small, satisfied sounds as she maneuvered him beside her. She pressed her head to his chest, bit his nipples playfully, and let her lips nip at the hair of his belly, making her way south. She licked hard at the underside of his shaft, took the dark head of his cock in her mouth, and worked him until he squirmed.

Tag pulled her face back up to his and kissed her deeply as he guided himself inside her with one hand. She locked her thighs around his hips, and they began a slow, steadily increasing undulation that soon became a thrashing of limbs, her pubic bone grinding against his.

"Max, Max," Giesla moaned. She came and bit his shoulder to keep from crying out, and on their next thrust, he followed her.

They lay for many minutes still joined, until Giesla came back to time and said, "I think we only have this room by the hour."

"You don't think Ham and Fruits will be using it, do you?" Tag said in her ear.

Giesla laughed softly. "I think I saw Francisco looking at one of the horses," she said. "And he is a very strange man."

"Well," said Tag, rising on his elbows, "never let it be said that I stood between a man and his love of nature. Let's get dressed."

"Yes," said Giesla, "but I am not leaving this warm place too soon."

"I've got a jar of Nescafe in my gear," Tag said. "You want some coffee?"

"And just a little of that plum wine to go with it," Giesla replied.

Tag got dressed, and when he returned with the wine, Giesla had remade the cot and lit the gas lantern. Tag made coffee from the water left in the kettle, gave Giesla the cup full of wine he had brought, and they sat down on the floor, resting against Tag's duffel bag, holding their stockinged feet toward the stove.

"Max," Giesla said, "tell me what is going on. I want to know everything."

"That guy Dzhukov, Yeshev's S-2, he's got a pile of reports you can go through. Sure you trust me to get it right?"

Giesla shrugged, sipped the wine, and said, "You are an undisciplined roughneck, Max. I told you that the first day we met."

"I remember."

"But you are not a bad soldier—for a cowboy. I think this once I will trust you."

Tag told her all he knew, including his own concerns and misgivings about the situation, and said, "So, what do you think?"

"We have seen worse," she said, "but this is not good. How soon do you think the Terrapin crews can be ready to begin conducting patrols?"

"We could squeeze the gunnery classes to make them patrols," he said. "Tambur and a couple of the others could go now, I think. If we shanghaied Ham and a couple of Yeshev's herd, plus you and me, we might be able to put ten effectives in the field tomorrow, in two-, three-, or five-patrol rotations, or as one small strike force."

Giesla shook her head. "No, Max, patrols. Intelligence is what worries me. We had such an advantage in the satellite images and aerial photos when we worked in the Jura. I feel so blind here, especially having to rely on the Mongols and the Russians."

"Not getting paranoid, are you?"

"No. I trust them, but I do not trust their systems or their intelligence apparatus."

"You're really worried, aren't you?"

"I hate to say, but, yes, that is my intuition."

"Well," said Tag, "maybe you are wrong." But he knew she seldom was.

6

The snow returned that night and fell steadily for three days. It was not truly a blizzard or even a storm, but the threat of its getting worse kept Tag's Terrapin crews within a couple of kilometers of camp. There was plenty of opportunity for the gunnery practice they needed, but none for patrols.

Giesla grew increasingly fretful over their lack of intelligence, and on the morning of the third day, with the snowfall showing signs of abating, she surprised Tag with a novel idea.

He was just a few hundred meters outside the perimeter, monitoring Ham's class on run-and-gun firing, when Giesla glided up beside the No Slack Too on a pair of skis.

"Max," she said, "I think I may have found a solution to our intelligence problem."

"No," he said, leaning farther out his hatch to give her the once-over, "you can't be serious."

"I have now four pair of skis," she said, ignoring his remark. "Zig and Dmitri have received permission to accompany me. Do you wish to be the fourth?"

"What, exactly, do you have in mind?"

"Just an out-and-back patrol. We see whether there is anything to see, then return."

Tag saw that she was determined, and he had no sound reason for refusing to let her go, especially if Yeshev had given his okay. What's more, if pressed, he would have to admit that he was getting antsy himself, more than ready for anything that would take him outside the perimeter. It had been years since he had cross-country skied, but he had always enjoyed it. And she was right: it was the only immediate way they had to gather first-hand information about what was happening out on the winter plains.

Tag took the No Slack Too back inside the perimeter, lashed on a pair of the antique hickory skis that Giesla had scrounged, armed himself with his 9mm automatic and a CAR-15 with a grenade launcher attachment, collected maps and binoculars, and skimmed out of the perimeter, heading southeast, at the head of the ad hoc patrol.

The snow was sifting down lightly. There was no wind, and the temperature had risen to minus-three degrees centigrade. It took Tag the first two kilometers to find his rhythm, and by then his thigh muscles were burning with his wasted effort. At the first opportunity, he led them up a knoll where an *ao bao* stood and stopped there on the excuse of wanting to con the area with his glasses.

There wasn't much to see, but Tag took his time, panning slowly across the landscape and flexing his legs to keep them loose. The best he could do to justify the halt was to plot a line of movement for them that would take advantage of what high ground there was, without too many slopes to climb.

He pushed off the knoll, crouched to gather speed, liking the bite of cold on his face, and let his momentum carry him halfway up the slope of the line of high ground he intended to follow. At the top, all four of them settled once again into a rhythmical, gliding stride, and Tag covered the next five kilometers more comfortably than he had the first three. Except for the soft sound of their skis, it was a silent world, windless and muffled by the falling blanket of snow. When the ridge that they had been following played out, Tag took them through a drifted swale and up to the top of another bald knoll, where a tumbled *ao bao* provided a good place to rest.

While Dmitri and Zig passed a thermos cup of tea, and Giesla adjusted the snowshoe bindings on her skis, Tag took out his maps and binoculars. They were now nearly one-third of the way to the drop zone where he and Yeshev had destroyed the Chinese parachute company, and that alone put his senses on alert. Added to that, there was the topography of the land immediately ahead of them. A series of parallel ridges ran across their path, providing low ground in between that would lend itself well to the advance of armor or large units of infantry—natural, if somewhat predictable, routes of approach to the flank of the Mongol-Russian line.

"Zig, Dmitri," he said, "listen up. We're going to be crossing four or five more crests"—he pointed to them in the distance—"and there could be anything on the other side, so I don't want anybody going over until we see what's there. We'll halt before we get to the top, and no one goes over until I give the word. You understand?"

"We understand, Captain," said Dmitri. He handed Tag the thermos cup of tea. "Between the tops, do you order that I should be drag?"

Tag took a drink and nodded. "But if the snow gets heavier, close in. We can't afford to get anyone lost out here."

He lifted the handset from the radio that Zig had set on the ground, reported their position to Minski, then led Zig and Giesla forward toward the first ridge.

They ran well, gliding on momentum off the knoll and all the way to the base of the ridge. From there, the wax on their hickories held traction to within twenty meters of the military crest. Tag crab-walked the last few feet on his mittened fists, ski poles dragging, and pulled his eyes above the horizon three inches away.

The fall of ground between this and the next ridge was not so great and much flatter. But the air was blurred with sifting snow, and Tag scanned every quadrant in his field of vision before he was certain there was no movement. He called up Giesla and Zig and had them do the same, before they all tipped over the crest and ran down a long slope. They pumped hard across the flat at the bottom, breathing hard beneath their knitted masks and the cowls of their parkas, and worked hard up the long slope opposite, flopping gratefully into the snow at the top. Each of them sensed the same thing, that they were deep in operational space now, and getting deeper, without any hope of support from camp. Everything mattered now.

Tag peered over the feathery crest and had begun working his elbows into the snow, getting comfortable, when he saw the movement through the gray haze of falling snow. It startled him how close it was. Less than a hundred meters away were more than a dozen figures putting on packs and tugging at the bindings of their snowshoes. He heard a snatch of language that he recognized as Chinese.

Tag slipped slowly down the slope, two meters below the crest, and motioned Zig and Giesla up beside him.

Using hand-and-arm signals, Tag told them what he had seen, and sent Giesla back up to the crest to keep an eye on the infiltrators. He took off one mitten, fished the strobe out of a cargo pocket inside his parka, and flashed a signal to Dmitri. He motioned for Zig to stay put, then crept back up the slope beside Giesla.

Tag eased his binoculars into position. From this distance, he could make out each man's features, his weapon and equipment. There were eighteen of them in all, each with a folding-stock AK carbine. All but two carried large field-transport packs, and of the two, one carried a battle pack and a radio, and the other only a pack. It wasn't hard for Tag to guess who was in command. They were all on their feet now, checking out one another's harnesses, stomping in the snow, ready to move out.

It was too good an opportunity for Tag to pass up. The situation wasn't right for a pure snatch, but Tag did owe

Menefee a prisoner or two, and things looked pretty good for that. Being outmanned more than four-to-one was no problem. He had speed, maneuverability, surprise, a knowledge of the terrain—and it was good terrain for what he needed. By the time Dmitri reached them, Tag had his plan.

It took only a minute to explain what he had in mind. The two Russian tankers, already familiar with those tank tactics of Ross Kettle's that were modeled on American Indian practices, were in vigorous agreement. They moved out parallel to the Chinese line of march, staying below the crest of the ridge, while Tag and Giesla crept back to the top.

When the Chinese column was fifty meters on their march, Tag signaled Giesla over the top. She tipped into the slope, crouched low over her bindings, her CAR-15 at the ready, and sailed through the fog of falling snow as silently as a wraith, while Tag covered her, the grenade launcher beneath the barrel of his carbine locked and loaded. With Giesla safely behind the first low rise of the farther ridge—and the Chinese now two hundred meters away—Tag waved to Dmitri and Zig and sidestepped over the crest, dropping instantly into a crouch. In the flat between the rises, he straightened and, firing across his body, popped a 40mm fragmentation round from the grenade tube.

The Chinese column paused at the sound, but before they could locate it, the grenade reached them. It passed through thirty inches of powder snow before it hit ice and detonated, killing one man instantly and wounding two others. The wounded screamed, and the officer barked out orders, as the Chinese troops scrambled into a defensive formation.

Tag gave them ten seconds to panic, then hit them with a second grenade. The Chinese radioman went down, his set smashed and his legs ripped by shrapnel. The Chinese began to return fire in Tag's general direction. He let the CAR-15 drop on its sling, took up the poles dangling from his wrists, and sprinted for the cover of the folded ridge.

He had less than fifty meters to cover but was nevertheless relieved to hear the rattle of fire from Dmitri and Zig cut loose behind the Chinese. Then, as he came out of the open, he heard Giesla open up from higher on the ridge. A Chinese round kicked snow inches from his skis, and then he was safe, churning his legs and arms and moving past Giesla, onto the reverse slope. The deep powder gave his skis a lot of bite, and he moved swiftly along the slope, parallel to the ridge, for a hundred meters, paused to listen to the shooting, then side-hopped to the crest and took up a firing position.

As Tag extended the stock of his carbine, slipped off one mitten, and took the pistol grip in his Thermex-gloved hand, he was already spotting his targets. The Chinese were scattered in a loose circle, about a hundred and fifty meters from him, obviously confused by the ambush. They were using their large transport packs for parapets, and that made it easier for him to pick them out through the snow. He settled the short metal stock of the CAR-15 into the thick shoulder of his parka, let his sight picture slide down from the horizon onto his first target, and tripped a three-shot burst.

The man screamed, flopped from behind the pack, dug at the snow with one twisted snowshoe, then lay still as a crystallizing red stain spread from his mouth.

Tag had his second man in his sights before the first was dead. He hammered out another burst, then immediately ripped a longer one into a position where two of the Chinese had thrown down their packs together.

The Chinese returned fire and began to shift their positions to cover Tag, but he was already on the move, and as he moved, Zig, Giesla, and Dmitri all opened up again from new positions. Tag scrabbled back up to the crest, peeked over, lined up a shot for the grenade launcher, and took out two more Chinese, whom he caught on their feet, trying to get out of the fire from his previous position. He followed that with a half dozen shots from his 9mm, just to give the Chinese something else to think about, then dropped below the crest and moved another twenty meters, before he looked over to survey the situation through his binoculars.

It had been like shooting hogs in a pen. Tag quickly counted ten dead and no more than four or five effectives remaining among the infiltrators. He could see the radio still on the back of one of the men lying apart from those still fighting. A figure broke toward the radioman, and Tag reached for his weapon. By the time he found his sights, the running man had gone to his belly, but still lay in the open. Tag shot for his extended legs. The man jerked over on one shoulder, reaching for his legs and writhing in pain.

Tag jacked another round into the grenade tube and was beginning to take aim, when one of the men in the group of effectives held up a rifle with a white rag tied to the folding stock. Tag saw a figure—either Zig or Dmitri—glide down the opposite ridge, and he came over the top himself, keeping the grenade launcher charged and at the ready.

Four men were on their feet when Tag and Dmitri closed on them, followed shortly by Giesla and Zig, who checked out the bodies. The man Tag had shot in the legs, the commander of the unit, was still alive, as was one other, who was unconscious but unmarked.

"Giesla," Tag said, "put some patches on these guys. Zig, Dmitri, have the rest of them rig up some stretchers. These guys are for the colonels."

While Giesla and the two Russians got the prisoners ready to move, Tag inspected the packs and equipment. In addition to the usual field gear, each of the packs contained various pieces of antitank ordnance—armor-piercing rocket-propelled grenades, shaped-charge land mines, and a total of ten anti-aircraft missiles and two launchers, also suitable for use against tanks.

Tag made a quick inventory as he dragged the packs together and dumped their contents in a pile, handing out the tents and poles to make litters and sorting out any letters, documents, or maps. When he was done, he took an RPG launcher and two of the grenades and rejoined the others.

"Ready to travel?" he asked. The four Chinese who could walk had the two wounded slung in the litters.

"Ready," said Giesla.

Tag led them all back to the top of the rise, where he stopped and fixed one of the RPGs on its launcher.

"Keep your heads down," he said.

Tag took aim on the pile of ordnance he had left stacked in the low ground, added some Kentucky windage, and ignited the RPG. The rocket motor hissed and sizzled off the end of the stick, corkscrewed, spun into stability, and arched into the hollow, falling ten meters short of the target.

"Round two," Tag said, twisting the second RPG into place. He added another degree of elevation, released the rocket, and the pile went up with crushing suddenness, showering the slopes of the rises with hot fragments of pack frames and shell casings.

It was slow going with the prisoners, but Tag lay an easier route for their return, one faster for men on snow-shoes than traversing all the same ridges. Still, it was late afternoon before they were within sight of the bivouac. Ham and Fruits in the No Slack Too, leading a formation of four Terrapins, met them a kilometer from the wire and carried the patrol and the prisoners back inside the compound.

Once inside the operations tent, with Giesla, Yeshev, Minski, and Dzhukov, Tag said, "They are going to hit the flank; I'm sure of it. Those guys we hit are not the only ones like them out there. They were moving into position to interdict our support movement, cut us out of the game, maybe even make a move on us here. Colonel," he turned to Yeshev, "I think we need to break camp."

Yeshev drew a long face and shook his head. "I do not have those orders," he said, "but I agree; it is time for us to act. I have been cornered once before, Captain, as you may remember, and I do not wish it again." He spoke to Major Minski. "Pavel," he said, "radio command and report on Captain Tag's patrol. Tell them we urgently request authorization to begin operational movement."

As Minski turned toward the radios of the communication center, Ham Jefferson sprang into the tent and called to Tag, "Hey, Bossman, Fruits has got a burp that just came in for you. The computer's printing it out now."

"Words or pictures?" Tag asked.

"Pretty pictures," Ham said.

Tag double-timed across the compound and was back with the images in five minutes.

There were two sets of pictures, one from satellite, and one from Stealth radar. What both showed, however, was evidence of large-scale armored movement in the middle of the snowstorm, all of it converging on the western flank of the main line of defense. The pictures were just eighteen hours old.

On the other hand, the response Minski had received from command reported a Chinese probe in the center of the line and a brief exchange of fire between armored units in that area, and Yeshev's orders were ambiguous.

"What do you suppose 'all necessary measures' means, Captain?" Yeshev asked Tag.

"My Russian isn't very good," said Tag, "but I think that means we can't attack if we're sitting still, and that a moving target is harder to hit than one that isn't."

"An excellent translation. Full alert, then." He turned to Minski and said, "Pavel, I want everyone ready to move out in two hours. Don't bother to strike the tents, but have the support units ready to leave by truck convoy to the north. They will move the prisoners, if we must evacuate this position."

As Minski went to pass along the order, Yeshev turned to Tag and said, "Now, we have some plans to make."

With Minski's help, they devised a battle plan that had the main body of Yeshev's ragtag regiment swinging into positions to blunt any Chinese thrust that would carry them past the flank and into the rear of the Mongol lines, while Tag and the Terrapins moved in from what would then be the Chinese flank. Yeshev made a final appeal to command for air-support priority and was given word to wait.

Giesla came to the operations tent to report that she had finished a preliminary interrogation of the prisoners and gone over their maps and documents. She had not learned a lot, but none of it contradicted what Tag and Yeshev suspected. The Chinese were members of China's elite winter corps, specially trained and equipped for antitank warfare. The bivouac was marked on their maps.

"It is settled, then," said Yeshev. "I want all my command officers here at once and every gun loaded."

Tag rejoined his crew and called Titz and Captain Tambur for a briefing. There was some question about what to do with the ponies and about what to do with Titz, but in the end there were enough supernumerary Mongols to take the horses with the truck convoy, and Titz insisted he should ride in the turret of the No Slack Too.

"Hey," he said, hiking up his soiled pink cummerbund and wrapping his greasy parka around him, "got to be there or be square, Captain."

The message traffic through the operations center was heavy that evening, and Tag had little sleep before the unit moved out at 0300.

Tag led the formation of Terrapins in the No Slack Too, positioning himself in the middle and letting the smaller armor fan out in double echelon behind him, with Tambur anchoring the right flank and the next-best crew securing the "hinge," where Yeshev's and Tag's areas of responsibility intersected. The snow had stopped, and a few stars were becoming visible through the scattering overcast as Tag led his strike force forward.

At 0400, as Tag and the Terrapins were approaching the place where he had ambushed the Chinese just sixteen hours before, he got the first word that war was on: the Chinese had hit the center of the line with air and armor. And fifteen minutes after that, he hit the Chinese flank.

When the No Slack Too topped the knoll that Tag had chosen to reconnoiter from, the column of Chinese tanks and APCs appeared in the distance like stampeding buffalo. They were traveling in close formation, striking hard for the Mongol-Russian flank. Hoping to use speed and surprise to their advantage, the Chinese had no pickets on the wings. There were easily two hundred pieces of armor in the column, from what Tag could see.

He flashed a coded signal to his unit and to Yeshev over the radio, then gave the command for the Terrapins to come on line.

As the Mongols raced into position, Tag said to Ham, "Gunner's choice, Hambone. Pick out something big."

"Mark, spark, and set to bark," Ham replied.

"Do it," Tag said, and the 120mm crashed back in its carriage dampers as the integral propellant sabot screamed from the muzzle.

Through his IR scope, Tag saw a Chinese T-72 explode in flame.

"Mark," said Ham.

"Splash one; shoot two," said Tag.

Ham was on the money again, as a second ChiCom tank ruptured from internal explosions. But the column did not slow or turn a gun on the No Slack Too. Tag ordered the Terrapins to his left to move into firing positions, and inside a minute the 105s began to boom. With rounds now falling by the handful among their ranks, taking a serious toll of hits, the Chinese could not ignore the fire. A dozen tanks peeled off and began advancing on the Mongol positions.

Tag ordered the Terrapins to his right to open fire, and soon another detachment of Chinese tanks was occupied in trying to silence them. Tag ordered both sides of his line to collapse in the center, and at the same time instructed Ham to fire at each of the ChiCom elements, hoping to draw them toward him. It at least drew their fire. A salvo of explosions enveloped the XM-F4, and Giesla accelerated through the smoke and hissing snow, churning the tracks of the No Slack Too in a race for cover. Tanks from each of the Chinese elements broke after her.

Tag ordered the Terrapins to close up the line, converging on the Chinese. Ham didn't get another shot. The Terrapins fell on the Chinese from the sides and rear and allowed only three to make it back to the column.

Tag ordered the Terrapins to scatter and snipe, while he radioed to Yeshev what was happening.

Yeshev had also already made contact and could do no more than acknowledge Tag's transmission.

Armored combat on open terrain, even when that terrain is covered by snow, happens with stunning speed. By the time Tag had concluded his brief radio contact, the main body of the column had pulled past him, so he ordered Tambur's wing to move left and concentrate its fire with the rest of the Terrapins, while the No Slack Too remained in place to anchor their shifting line. He pressed forward, allowing Tambur to cut behind him, while Ham kept up a regular pounding of the ChiCom stragglers. He didn't see the second wave of armored infantry until a Panda antitank rocket flattened itself against the turret of the No Slack Too and seared a pock in the slick skin armor, rocking the crew inside with its delayed detonation.

"Cover our six," Tag shouted as his sensors picked up the mass of APCs and support armor just rounding into view from behind the ridge.

Fruits swung the Phalanx as Giesla turned the tank, and Ham locked on target, all in one motion. The No Slack Too came about firing. Tag primed the War Clubs and loosed a brace of them at the lead elements of the second wave, ripping a pair of burning holes in the Chinese formation. The Phalanx chopped the APCs like so much liver. Ham knocked out two tanks in rapid succession.

Titz, braced in the back of the turret and still a little dazed from the rocket's impact, shouted, "Go, go, go, go."

"Go, Giesla," said Tag. "Get us back to cover. Main tube right, Phalanx left. Shoot 'em if you got 'em."

With both guns blazing, one into the vanguard of the armored infantry, the other into the rear of the first column, the No Slack Too fishtailed through the loose snow and leaped forward out of the converging lines of fire.

Tag alerted his Terrapins to the approach of the second wave and directed Giesla into a fighting position in the saddle between two low knolls. His own ground radar and IR sensors gave Tag clear vision of the battlefield, and he was secure in the knowledge that the Chinese couldn't find him when he was sitting still and not firing. From his vantage in the crotch of the hills, he watched as confused and frightened skirmishers in old T-54 tanks prowled the near flank of the armored infantry column. As they reduced their interval from the rest of the column, Tag ordered Ham to take them, and in seconds both of the antiquated tanks sat in flames.

Tag's next position, the one he had located while Ham took out the T-54s, was to the right and nearly five hundred meters away, which would put more than a kilometer between the No Slack Too and the Terrapins. In any other tank, Tag might have thought twice, but he had confidence in their speed and in having open country to his rear in which he could fall back and lose any pursuit.

As Giesla swung them into position, Yeshev's voice came up on the TacNet: "Butcher Boy, Butcher Boy, this is Alpha Fox. Over."

"Butcher Boy here," Tag responded.

"Butcher Boy, everything is coming back to you. Everything. Do you copy? Over."

"Butcher Boy copy. Thanks, Alpha Fox."

"Alpha Fox out."

"We turned 'em, gang," Tag said to the crew. "Now, we've got to get out of their way and let 'em back through."

He twisted his scope to the north and, jacking up the magnification, saw what Yeshev had meant. In the eerie infrared glow of the scope, Tag could see a literal blot of retreating Chinese armor squeezing its way between the hills to the east and the guns of the Terrapins to the west. Then he saw the blot begin to spread into the gap between his own position and the Mongols'.

"Shit," he said. "Giesla, make for the bivouac—scratch that. Just take us west, best way you can."

Hundreds of ChiCom tanks and APCs were pouring back from their encounter with Yeshev's guns, pouring back and spreading out between Tag and the Terrapins. Giesla felt as though she were racing to outrun a tidal wave, so she ran that hard, pushing the No Slack Too up on its suspension, forcing the turbines to the max. Twice Chinese tanks passed within close range, but neither they nor Tag paused to fight. He had no fear of any armor on earth, one-on-one, but given enough of them, even ducks could peck you to death.

7

The cyclonic cloud began to gather in western Gansu Province, near the farthest reach of the Great Wall. The tiny dust devils that it spawned danced across the cold-desiccated earth, skipped through tumbled gaps in the Great Wall, coalesced, and merged again with the clouds. The rotation spread through the lower atmosphere, as the storm's own momentum gave it size and it drew strength from the trough of low pressure that sucked it toward Mongolia. Over the southern Gobi, it lifted acres of fine dust and sand that trapped moisture from the heavy air and froze, clumping together to fall like hail. When the freezing sand struck any object, any man, any camel, it stuck and began to accumulate. Legend has it that entire caravans have been locked in rictus by the freezing sandstorms of the Gobi, discovered like macabre statuary, frozen on the Silk Road to Cathay.

The No Slack Too raced to escape the torrent of retreating Chinese, straight toward the approaching storm.

What had begun as a stinging counterstrike by Yeshev's regiment against the enveloping Chinese quickly turned into a rout. Already hurt and distracted by the Terrapin ambush, the Chinese were easy prey for Yeshev's crack troops. There was nothing exotic about the battle. Yeshev had superior intelligence and the element of surprise, and he used them to perfection, smashing the ChiCom column with a withering fire from cover. Units from the main defensive line were shifted to support the flank, and thirty minutes after the first shot, the Chinese armor was falling back on its own infantry. The collision of those forces shattered them, and they spread out into the desert like rats boiling from a flooded sewer.

Each time Tag thought he could order his tank back north toward the bivouac, he spotted more Chinese tanks and APCs that he would have to cross. And each time he considered blasting his way through, he thought of two things. The first was military: he didn't know how many Chinese there were to the north or exactly where they were. The second was folk wisdom: an old sergeant-major he had known, who was prone to brawling in bars, once told Tag, "Never fight a coward, son. You get one of them sons of bitches in a corner, and he'll kill you trying to get out."

He was so intent on keeping tabs on the scattered Chinese and on searching out a route back to their base that Tag paid no notice to the shifting patterns of clouds above him. Even when he halted the XM-F4 on a knoll and climbed up through the turret to stand in the hatch and scan the terrain, he did not contemplate the curving fish-gill clouds piling in from the west or the low, dark band across the western horizon.

Tag slid down from the turret and into his seat and said over the intercom, "Okay, gang, we're through screwing around. This is no longer a withdrawal. It's a recon patrol. We're going to make a sweep through the desert, out there where there's not supposed to be anything. Eventually, we'll be shed of those Chinese, and we can maybe beat Freddy and the boys back to camp. Anybody that needs to make a pit stop, do it now."

When everyone was settled back inside, Tag gave Giesla the LandNav coordinates for their objective—on the map, a small cluster of buildings beside a government-built reservoir. As an objective, its only virtues were that it was at the very edge of the desert, where no Chinese tank would intentionally go, and that the getting there was all over level ground. With Ham and Fruits holding the weapons ready, Giesla let the turbines whine, aimed them for the open west, and dropped the No Slack Too in gear.

The morning brightened only to gray that day, and at first Tag thought he had hit some sort of haze, but nothing he could do would clear the optical scope or the VCR camera, and he was getting balky responses to anything with an exterior link, including his radio.

"How's your visibility?" he asked Giesla.

"Terrible," she said.

"Hold up. I want to take a look."

Tag threw back the dogs on his hatch and stuck his head out. Pellets of frozen sand hit his Kevlar IV helmet like so many BBs, sticking to the camouflage fabric covering it. Tag pulled his head back in and called up through the turret, "Titz, put your head out and tell me what the hell this is."

Tag heard the turret hatch clang back, then Titz called down to him, "Bad shit, honcho. Freezing sand. We need to get where you want to be, because in thirty minutes, this bucket of bolts is going to be yard art—concrete, man, rock solid."

Tag was already tugging a Thermex mask over his face. "I'm going to ride with the window open," he said, popping his goggles into place. "Just follow the LandNav, Gies. If I see anything, I'll tell you. Let's move it."

Tag had to paw continually at his goggles to keep them clear of the sand that pelted his head and shoulders as he rode in the open commander's hatch, and the sand that caught in the weave of his mask gave him the horrible sensation of choking, so that he had to lift the bottom of it to breathe while he scraped away the frozen veneer. His sole consolation was in knowing that any Chinese who strayed this far were having it just as rough.

The pitch of the turbines changed, and a shudder ran through the No Slack Too.

"What's happening, Gies?" he mumbled into the intercom through his stiffening mask.

"We're losing power," she said. "The air intakes must be clogging."

"Fruits," Tag said, "shinny out on the rear deck. Take something with you to chip ice."

"Aw, fuck me," Fruits whined as he opened the turret hatch. He moved from handhold to handhold, using the radio mast and the cleats for reactive armor to brace himself, until he could reach the snorkels with the screwdriver he carried. He held on with one hand and hacked at the brown crudesence around the intakes.

"Hey, Captain Max," he said to Tag through the intercom, "this ain't workin' for shit. I'm gonna have to use the de-icer."

The de-icer was in a cylinder like a fire extinguisher and was intended for emergency thawing of moving parts, but Tag could see no bigger emergency than getting stuck in the Gobi in a freezing sandstorm.

"Do it," he said. "Do whatever you have to, but keep us moving."

The No Slack Too had been less than thirty kilometers from the reservoir when the first grains of sand stuck to its armor, but the last ten had seemed to Tag to take forever. Fighting his own battle with visibility and asphyxiation, he had to swallow a lump in his throat each time the turbines stuttered, and he began to see things that were not there, once mistaking a growing clot of sand on the fringe of his parka for a boulder, and once experiencing a brownout, his vision losing all focus in the sweeping sand. He turned away to clear the goggles, blinked, and saw a gust of wind plaster a layer of brown ice on the leading edge of the track skirt, the way blown concrete builds up the side of a swimming pool.

"Can you see it yet?" Giesla asked, her voice booming inside Tag's helmet. "The LandNav has us there."

Tag whipped his head from side to side, trying to keep from facing directly into the wind, and caught a glimpse of right angles, the corner of something man-made.

"A little to your left," he said. Tag navigated Giesla into the lee of a mud-brick building set beside the loose rock wall of a corral. A half-dozen woolly yaks huddled behind a part of the building that extended into the corral, but Tag could see no other sign of life. Now out of the wind himself, he could hear the pellets of frozen sand tattooing the tiled roof of the building, could see the accumulation on the rock fence.

"Ham, Fruits," Tag said, "go naked and check this place out. Take your strobes with you. You could get lost ten feet away in this shit."

The gunner and loader piled out through the turret hatch and clambered, slipping and cussing, off the rear deck, disappearing into the storm and around the corner of the building.

Titz, who had followed them out of the hatch, came to the front of the tank and said to Tag, "This is bad noogie, amigo. You got to get your machine under cover."

Irritated by the obvious, Tag ignored Titz and climbed out the hatch, dragging his CAR-15 behind him. He slid over the glacis, its surface roughened with frozen sand, hit the snow at a crouch, and straightened up to look directly into the half-curious, half-frightened face of a Mongol boy of ten or so, who stood at the intersection of the rock corral and the wall of the building, peering from the hood of a woolly parka.

Titz followed Tag's eyes, saw the boy, and rattled out something in rapid Mongolian. The boy replied, then Titz turned to Tag and said, "See? Even the boy says the same thing."

"Who else is here?" Tag said, suddenly alert, tightening his grip on his rifle.

Titz and the boy exchanged words, and the translator said, "He says just his family. They live here through the winter. In the spring the farmers come to raise wheat."

"Did you tell him who we are, that we're friends?"

"He knows that," said Titz. "He just wants to know why you're leaving this fine machine sitting outside."

Tag wondered whether Titz was a Chinese agent sent to torment him. "Goddammit, Titz, ask him where we can put it."

Titz spoke to the boy, who disappeared around the building.

"He says he will ask his father," Titz said.

Ham and Fruits came back into the lee of the building, covered in what looked like globular, sparkling mud. Ham peeled the mask back off his face, spat, and said, "Well, we got us some chow and a roof. You done anything for me recently?"

Tag grinned and rapped on Giesla's hatch. "Hmm," he hummed. "Well, Hambone, I haven't court-martialed you yet."

As Giesla emerged through the driver's hatch, the boy returned with a man too young to be his father. The man spoke to Titz, who turned to Tag and said, "You follow him. He's got a place for the tank."

"Ham," said Tag, "you and Fruits go ahead. We'll get the Too stashed and meet you for lunch."

As Tag climbed back through his hatch, he heard a small gasoline engine start somewhere nearby. He and Giesla crept along in the No Slack Too, following the young man, until they reached a solitary concrete pole with an electric line running into a small metal box on its side. The young Mongol took a small brass-handled dagger from his waist, chipped at the box, opened it, threw a switch, and with a strained whine of electric motors, the earth opened before them. Tag got a whiff of fermented grain and knew at once what it was—an underground silo for the grain raised here in the summers. This late in the winter it would be nearly empty. It stank like nothing else in the world, but it was deep, safe, and warm inside. Besides, although the No Slack Too could do a lot, it couldn't smell.

Tag couldn't make out the dimensions of the complex of buildings that the young Mongol led them to, once the No Slack Too was sealed underground, but he had the impression that they were large. And when they got inside, he was certain. The mud-brick and stucco compound was a sprawl, a hive, a warren, with rooms letting off each other in every direction. The large room that they first entered was warm, lit by gas lanterns, and filled with Mongols of every age who were talking, sewing clothes, mending saddle harnesses, drinking tea, napping, and generally going about their lives with minimal notice of Tag and his crew of big-nosed foreigners.

A wiry man with a weathered face came forward and spoke to Tag in Mongolian, extending one hand to him and gesturing to the room with the other.

Titz said, "He welcomes you and your warriors, Captain. He says you are honored guests. His name is Hangay. You want some grub?"

"Thank him for me, Titz," said Tag. "Tell him we are in his debt and that we could use some food."

Titz spoke to Hangay, who turned and spoke to two teen-age girls. They giggled, got off the low stucco platform where most of the extended family was sitting, and went into the adjoining room.

Hangay spoke again to Titz, who turned to Tag and said, "Come on, Captain. Let's grab a seat and toast our buns."

They all sat on the carpet-covered platform, which was part of the flue for the stove in the next room, warmed by the smoke passing through it. The women and children made room for them, and one grandmother passed a basket of the sour-sweet dried yogurt.

Tag and the crew smiled and nodded and generally tried to show their appreciation for the Mongols' hospitality. In a few minutes, the two girls returned with a tin kettle of the smoky tea, some barley gruel, and a platter of tough mutton.

Between mouthfuls, Tag said to Titz, "Hey, Titz, ask Hangay whether there's been any Chinese movement out here in the past few days, anything we might need to know."

"A done deal," said Titz. He spoke with the Mongol elder for several minutes, while Tag listened, hoping he might catch something. He didn't, however, and was growing impatient when Titz finally turned back to him.

"Well, Captain," the translator said, "looks like everything hasn't been so quiet on the western front."

"What do you mean, Titz? Give it to me straight."

Titz belched, hiked up his cummerbund, took a sip of tea, and said, "It's like this: about a week ago the old guy here and one of the boys were out rounding up their doggies, and they were braced by a Chinese patrol. Nothing came out of it, though. Then, two days ago, the same patrol came through here. They offered to buy a couple of sheep with Chinese money. The old man told them no, so they took them. He's real pissed about that and wants to know if we can get his sheep back."

"Does he have any idea where the patrol went, where it is now?"

After a brief exchange with Hangay, Titz said, "He's not sure, but he thinks they may be working out of a dugout shelter a couple of kilometers from here, unless they've moved out of the area."

Tag grunted and said, "Okay. At least they're not going to be out in this. We'll ride the storm out, then see if Hangay can point us toward the dugout. Not much else to do that I can see."

While the storm raged and swirled outside, Tag and his

crew found time to relax with their hosts. With all the interconnected rooms of the compound and all the coming and going among them, it was hard to estimate how many people made up the extended family, but Tag supposed at least twenty. The younger children were fascinated by Ham Jefferson's dark skin, and they would sneak up to touch him, then pull away, giggling behind their hands, while he made monster faces at them, to everyone's delight. Fruits played paper-stone-scissors with some of them, and Giesla admired the needlework that the women were applying to the hems of their coats and dresses. Hangay and the young men produced their collection of weapons—knives, a bow, cheap shotguns, and one antique but immaculate 7mm Mauser—for which Tag showed a proper appreciation. And when the Mongols learned that his family raised cattle and horses in the high plains of America, he quickly found himself swapping yarns, through Titz's eccentric translations, about blizzards, lost stock, and memorable horses.

By mid-afternoon, the storm had passed, leaving behind a landscape pebbled with the frozen sand and a sky of light gray overcast, with the temperature hovering just a few degrees below zero centigrade. Tag and Giesla went out to check on the No Slack Too, which sat in the silo up to its track skirts in reeking silage, but safe and secure. Less than five minutes after they had returned to the living quarters, the boy Tag had first met by the corral came rushing in to say that there were soldiers approaching, Chinese soldiers.

"How many?" Tag asked Titz.

"Same patrol," Titz said. "About a baker's dozen."

"Let's get to the tank," said Tag.

"No time, honcho," Titz told him. "Hangay wants you all to go with the boy there. He's got a place you can hide."

"Okay, people," Tag said, "get your gear. Don't leave anything that says we're here, and come with me."

The boy led them into a pantry off the kitchen and opened a trapdoor to a root cellar.

"Aw, man," Fruits whined, "I don't like this shit one bit."

"Be cool, Fruits Loops," said Ham. "We don't want to get our buddies here shot up. We get down here in the dark and you can go off in the corner and play with yourself."

"Aw, fug you," Fruits said. He threw his gear into the cellar and went down the short ladder after it.

Once they were all inside, Tag positioned himself with his CAR-15 on the ladder and motioned for the boy to drop the door. There was nothing for him to see through the cracks between the boards, but the boy left the pantry door open, and Tag could at least hear anyone approaching.

Like each of the others in the cellar, all he could hear at first was the sound of his own pulse thrumming in his ears. But after some minutes he did hear the sounds of feet hitting the floor, followed by voices speaking in Chinese. He felt Giesla pressing against his leg as she leaned in to listen. Figures passing the door to the pantry cast shadows across the trapdoor. There was more talking, then the sounds of heavy boots again, followed by the creaking of the hinges on the front door.

The activity in the living quarters subsided, although Tag could still hear people in the kitchen just off the pantry, the opening and closing of the stove, the rattle of cooking pots. Through a crack between the boards on the trapdoor, he could see the back of a girl's head. She moved aside, and a figure in a white winter uniform came into view. He spoke in Chinese, barked out a laugh, and left.

Tag's eyes had adjusted enough to the darkness that he could see the others standing below him. He handed his carbine down to Giesla and slipped from its sheath his tulip-shaped fighting knife with the deep blood grooves. He held it so Ham and Fruits could see, and they responded by pulling their own blades and moving into position at the foot of the ladder. A kettle in the kitchen began to sing, and Tag pushed back the door to the cellar, holding it for Ham and Fruits to follow.

With all three of them in the pantry, Tag let the door down gently and listened. The girl at the stove had not heard him. He hissed at her and when she turned, he held his finger to his lips for silence. He tried to put on a questioning look and began holding up fingers, to ask how many Chinese there were. The girl looked at him for a moment without comprehending, then recognition dawned on her face. She held up two fingers and pointed to the other room, then held up all ten fingers and made a motion to indicate that the others were either gone or, at least, outside.

Tag turned to Ham and Fruits and passed along the information with his hands, then motioned for Ham to follow and moved along the wall into the kitchen.

Tag stopped beside the connecting doorway. He could hear the two Chinese talking casually in the next room and tried to visualize the layout, to picture in his mind where they were and determine whether they were alone. No luck. He looked to the girl, who was keeping her back to him while she worked at the stove, and hissed at her. She looked over one shoulder, and Tag nodded to the steaming kettle, making a motion with one hand as though he were dropping something. The girl swallowed and bobbed her head. She lifted the kettle, held it away from her, gave a cry, and let it crash to the floor.

The Mongol woman who came first through the door went past Tag and Ham without noticing them. Then Tag heard the sounds of approaching boots. The ChiCom soldier stepped through the door and stopped. Before he could speak, Tag had one arm around the man's throat and a knife in his kidney. The pain was so intense that the man could not even cry out. Tag leaned back, holding the man's feet off the floor, and twisted the blade deeper, hot blood running over the back of his hand.

Ham moved past Tag and met the second Chinese with a straight right that sent the man tumbling back over his heels, out cold. Ham was on him instantly, his knife going for the throat.

"Wait," Tag shouted. "Tie him and gag him, Ham. We want a prisoner out of this bunch." He jerked his blade out of the man he held, twisting him as he fell, and cut his throat with a single slash, mixing blood with the boiling water from the kettle on the floor.

Titz appeared in the doorway, saying, "Far out, big kahuna."

Tag wiped his blade on the dead man's uniform and said, "Where are the others?"

"They split," Titz said. "From what I heard, it sounds like they're going to get some of their pals and bring them up this way."

"How many?"

"Ten."

"No, how many are they bringing up?"

"Beats me."

"Shit," Tag said. "Listen, Titz, you tell these people that they need to get the hell out of here. When those guys get back, they're gonna be real pissed about their buddies."

"I'll tell them," Titz said, "but they'll do what they want. You know how Mongols are; you can't tell us anything."

"Just do it."

The quarters were full of activity again. Hangay was simultaneously pounding Tag on the back and shouting orders to the others, who were dragging off the body and cleaning up the mess in the kitchen, stripping clothes and weapons off the unconscious Chinese, and producing their own guns from cupboards and closets.

Giesla came up from the cellar and said, "What is happening, Max?"

"The patrol has gone back out to make contact with another unit and bring them here," he said. "And it looks like our friends here are planning to take them on, unless I can talk them out of it."

"Is that man alive?" she asked, pointing with the CAR-15 to the Chinese soldier on the floor.

"Yeah, unless Hambone has got more pop in his right than he used to have."

"Do I have time to talk to him?"

"Make it quick. You want Ham to help?"

"Yes," she said, smiling wickedly. "Sergeant Jefferson is very persuasive. And I will need Mr. Titz to translate."

"Do it," Tag said. "Fruits and I will go get the Too."

Giesla took a capsule of smelling salts from her medical pouch and snapped it beneath the nose of the unconscious Chinese.

He jerked away from it and began to come around.

"Ham, Titz," she said, "come here."

Ham and Titz hoisted the soldier into a chair, and the first thing he saw when he could focus his eyes was a leering black face six inches from his own. The man screamed and began to babble.

"He thinks you are a devil," said Titz.

"Well," said Ham, "you tell him that I am. Tell him that I eat Chinese raw, starting with the balls." He ran the tip of his knife along the inside of the man's thigh.

The man babbled something else in Chinese, and Titz said, "I think he believes you."

"Good," Giesla said, laying one hand on the man's neck and stepping behind him. "Now, you tell him that if he answers my questions, I may be able to save him. Tell him that Ham is my pet devil, but that lies drive him crazy. Ask him where the rest of the patrol went and what they are to do."

Titz exchanged words with the Chinese, then turned to Giesla and said, "He says he isn't sure."

"Too bad," said Giesla. "Ham."

Ham slit the man's trousers up the inseam, leaving a thin

line of blood on his flesh, then prodded none too gently at the base of his balls. The Chinese squealed in terror and squirmed in the chair. Giesla held his shoulders firmly.

"Ask him again," she said.

But Titz did not have to. The man began talking.

When Tag came back, the ChiCom soldier was still in the chair, clenching a towel to his thigh and staring in horror at Ham Jefferson, who was hunkered on his heels in front of him.

"Oh, bless my Geneva Conventions," said Tag. "I don't even want to know what you've been up to in here. What'd he have to say, Gies?"

"He has been very forthcoming, Max," she said. "He is part of an airborne unit that has orders to move on our bivouac. If the assault had been successful, they were only to occupy our position. Now, he thinks they will try to attack, catch us off guard."

"Hmm. Probably still hoping to stretch the main line thin and hit it again," Tag said. "How many in the main force?"

"About two hundred, all equipped with antitank weapons."

"And how far from here?"

"About that, he says he is not certain. He and the other man that they left here were told it would be two days— the day after tomorrow—before they were relieved."

"Okay," said Tag, "that's plenty for now. Let's get him loaded up and hiako. If we really cook, we can make it back before dark."

Tag thanked Hangay and his family again and urged them one last time to evacuate the compound, then loaded everyone in the No Slack Too, with Titz and the prisoner wedged in the rear of the turret, and laid a course for the bivouac, which they reached just before sundown, less than a half hour after the first Terrapins and elements of Yeshev's regiment had returned.

8

The Russians needed the victory, and their spirits were running high, but the Mongols under Captain Tambur were almost out of control. One of the Terrapins had been destroyed by Chinese fire, and another disabled, but between Tag's training and their own innate knack for guerrilla tactics, the Mongols had kicked some serious butt, with each of the surviving Terrapins chalking up at least one confirmed kill and Tambur himself claiming five.

"It was a crushing defeat for the Chinese," said Yeshev. He, Tag, Giesla, Minski, and Dzhukov were gathered in the operations tent, along with Titz and the Chinese captive. "We were in perfect position," the Russian colonel continued. "When the Chinese turned to sweep on the flank of the line, they put themselves directly under our guns. And your Terrapins had already confused them. They were not expecting us at all. We will get a complete after-action report from command, but during our sweep of the area after the Chinese fell back, I estimated between eighty and one hundred pieces of armor destroyed, and our troops were still taking prisoners when we withdrew."

"How many did you lose?" asked Tag.

Yeshev shrugged off his parka and rubbed his hands over the stove. "We had two mechanical failures," he said, "and we took some hits. I lost only one crew to fire, however."

"And why did you not remain on the field, Colonel?" Giesla asked.

"Command is still concerned about this sector, Lieutenant," Yeshev replied. "And your intelligence seems to confirm their suspicions. Tell me all about your little foray."

Tag leaned forward on his stool, put his elbows on his knees, and began a slow, detailed account of their day, ending with the observation that they ought to pump the prisoner a little more, before forwarding him on to command.

Yeshev nodded. "Command has given us greater latitude to plan and execute operations in this sector, Captain. If what you have already said is true, I believe that those operations should commence at once. Let us see what your prisoner can tell us."

Ham Jefferson had made such an impression on the captured Chinese that Giesla had no need to call him in for this interrogation. The threat was enough. Dzhukov, despite his relative youth and inexperience as an intelligence officer, proved a sharp cookie, instinctively playing the good cop to Giesla's hardcase role. Between them and Titz's disorienting three-way translations, Tag and Yeshev were convinced after an hour that the man had told them not only everything he knew—including his commander's love of pickled garlic—but everything he even suspected.

After the prisoner had been led off, Tag scratched his ear and said, "You know, if we believe what that little buzzard says, I have a sneaking suspicion that the entire flanking movement was itself a diversion, maybe even a calculated defeat."

"You do not believe that the Chinese wanted to lose, do you, Max?" Giesla asked.

"No, not exactly, Gies. My hunch is that it didn't matter whether they won or lost. If they won, they won, and that'd be an end to that. But if they lost, we would believe that the danger from the flank was past, maybe even abandon this position to support the main line and give them a clear avenue of approach."

"Approach across the Gobi?" Yeshev said. "Captain, you have just seen what the Gobi can do."

"I know," said Tag, "but the Chinese know the Gobi better than we do, know what to expect from it. We didn't think that they would move armor up in the winter, either, or that they would be able to attack coming out from under a blizzard. The more I see of them, the more I believe that the least likely thing is the very thing they will try."

Yeshev gestured toward the map board on the wall. "Well, Captain," he said, "we have thousands of square kilometers of unlikely. What would you choose?"

Tag studied the map, rose, and walked to it. "I was thinking while we came in that what we really need is aerial observation," he said, "but I know that is not going to be forthcoming, at least not in the intensity we need. And we can't cover everything with the Terrapins alone. But—and this is a big but—what if we put out pony patrols? This is the Mongols' home turf, so we supply them with radios and turn them loose to do what they do best."

"Captain," Yeshev said patronizingly, "this is the twenty-first century. Do you seriously propose that we resort to cavalry?"

"Is there a better way?"

"Comrade Colonel," said Minski, "I think there may be some merit to Captain Tag's idea. At least, I see no serious drawbacks. Men on horseback would be no less efficient than foot patrols, and they could cover much more country. After all, we are talking about reconnaissance, not strike forces."

"That's right," Tag said, "and even if the Chinese saw them, they would attract a lot less attention than tanks or Terrapins, maybe even pass for civilians."

Yeshev pondered all this for a moment, then said, "Can their ponies operate effectively in this snow?"

"It's not nearly as deep out there," Tag said, "maybe eight or ten inches, about twenty to twenty-five centimeters. That shouldn't be any problem. But why don't we ask Tambur?"

"Very well," said Yeshev. "Go talk to Captain Tambur, then come and tell me what you intend. Understand, however, that I can assign none of the regular battalion armor for this, unless there is an imminent attack."

"Understood," said Tag. "And thanks, Colonel. C'mon, Gies. Let's go."

Captain Tambur was excited by the proposal. He had more men than Tag had Terrapins, anyway, and he was only too ready to put them to use. And, Tag suspected, the Mongols were equally eager to show what they could do on horseback.

"Wondering," said Tambur. "This is wondering. How can we do for you?"

Tag turned to Titz, pulled a wry face, and said, "As much as I hate to admit it, I think I'm going to need your help here, Titz."

"Hey, it's a snap, honcho," Titz said.

Working late into the evening under a gas lantern in Tambur's yurt, he, Tag, and Giesla hammered out a patrol scenario. Ten of the Terrapins would be split into teams of two, each team radiating out from the bivouac to define sectors within which the men on horseback would operate. The No Slack Too and the remaining Terrapins would form the reaction force, moving out on a line that would take them back toward the known concentration of Chinese due to arrive at the compound by the reservoir. Beyond that, they would all have to play it by ear and hope that it was only airborne infantry they would encounter.

Tag was awakened early the following morning by the sounds of whinnying horses and shouting Mongols. And when he emerged from his yurt, he stopped in his tracks to witness a scene of hellish chaos, as dozens of Mongol ponies thrashed on the ground, surrounded by men with saddles and bridles who leaped like Cossack dancers to avoid the flailing hooves, while others tried to hold the horses still. The men who would be going out on the horses had shed their military uniforms in favor of the barbaric dress that Tag had seen at the victory party, complete with pointed felt hats trimmed in yak hair, embroidered woolen coats, and knee-high boots with wicked-looking spurs. But each man also had an AK-74 slung on his back and wore a patrol harness bulging with grenades and ammunition. Tag had never seen so many of the Mongols smiling all at once.

In a half hour, the patrols were set, and the teams of Terrapins rolled out of the perimeter, diverging for the horizon. The snow was crusted and dirty from the freezing sand, and the Terrapins left white tracks through it, as though their tires were vacuuming paths across a soiled carpet. When they were out of sight, Tag gave the order for the horsemen to move out, then headed up his strike force for the reservoir.

The temperature, though still below freezing, continued to be mild, and the sun felt good on Tag's back as he rode in the open turret hatch, with the eight remaining Terrapins in a staggered column behind, led by Captain Tambur, a Mongol gonfalon flapping from his antenna mast. Tag was especially glad to be able to ride outside, because he had had to bring Titz with him, to communicate with the Mongol patrols, and the weird translator was a long way from his last bath—probably in the fall. In the warmth of the turret, there was a distinct pong of garlic, mutton grease, and body odor. Tag had, however, found Titz easier to tolerate after the coolness he showed when the Chinese patrol arrived at the Mongol compound. If there was one thing that Tag had learned, it was that a man's courage couldn't be equated with his eccentricities or personal hygiene habits. Fruits Tutti had taught him that.

Tag halted his column two kilometers from the reservoir and sent one of the Terrapins forward to recon the area, in case the approaching Chinese had made better time than they had planned. But he got an all-clear signal from the Terp and pulled into the compound at midmorning.

The place appeared deserted. There were still yaks and goats in the pens and corral, but no ponies and no sign of the Mongol family. He ordered the Terrapins into a defensive perimeter and got down from the No Slack Too to investigate.

He walked around the outside of the rambling, mud-brick living quarters and poked his head into the barn and all the sheds, even inspected the entrance to the silo for signs of activity. Nothing. As he stood beside the stone corral, scratching his head and wondering where the family could have gone, a shout went up from the perimeter.

Tag sprinted for the No Slack Too but slowed to a walk when he saw what the shout was about. Six Mongols on horses were cantering across the frozen desert, with Hangay in the lead, his prized Mauser slung from the red-felt-covered saddle tree. Tag loped across the crusty brown snow, calling for Titz to come with him, and met Hangay and his boys as they entered the compound.

It took only a few minutes for Tag to learn what had happened. After the No Slack Too left, Hangay had decided that it might be too dangerous for the women and children, and he had evacuated them to the dugout shelter that the Chinese patrol had used, then returned with his two sons and three oldest grandsons. Hangay said he was very glad to have Tag back. The old Mongol looked over the Terrapins and their crews, spoke with Captain Tambur, and nodded his general approval.

"He wants to know," said Titz, "if he and his boys can fight in your horde."

"My what?" said Tag.

"You horde, man. You know, your gang, your army."

Horses, hordes, Mongols with Mausers—Tag was beginning to feel just a little disoriented by the course of events, always a good sign to him, when his instincts told him things were right.

"Yeah. Sure. Okay," he said. "Tambur can use them for local security or whatever."

"With pressure," said Captain Tambur.

"Also," Tag went on, "I want two Terps sent out to extend our own feelers. We already know that there is at least one Chinese unit headed this way. Let's don't let them see us first."

Titz translated, and Tambur and Hangay talked some more. Then, the translator said to Tag, "It's in the bag, kahuna."

"Titz," Tag said, "you say you learned English from American movies?"

"That's a fact."

"What's your favorite?"

"*Beach Blanket Bingo*," Titz said with a grin. "It's narly, dude."

Tag shook his head and walked back to the No Slack Too.

Patrol reports of Chinese movement began coming in less than an hour later, first from a pair of Terrapins, then from two different pony patrols, each sighting groups of eighty to one hundred men on foot carrying large packs.

"More airborne, Bossman?" Ham Jefferson asked.

"I reckon," said Tag. "Sounds like the same configuration. What I'm wondering now is how damn many of these infiltration units there are. If it's very many, we need to call in Freddy and the boys. Giesla, see if you can raise Yeshev on the hook. Tell him what we know so far, and see what he says."

While waiting for Yeshev's reply, Tag got another patrol report from his own two Terrapins. They had spotted the Chinese moving toward the compound, about a hundred of them, fifteen kilometers away. Then came another sighting, and follow-up reports coming from the first patrols to spot the Chinese told Tag that all these units were converging and would reach battalion strength between here and the bivouac, probably by this time tomorrow.

"What's the word from Freddy?" he said to Giesla, who was sitting in the driver's seat of the XM-F4 with her head out the hatch.

"They say that if we cannot engage, we are to fall back."

Tag's mind spun as he calculated their options. "Okay," he said, "put the word out to all our units that they are to keep up their observation, but no contact yet. It doesn't even matter if the ChiComs see them, as long as they stay out of range."

"What you got in mind, Boss?" Ham asked.

"Could I get you in the mood for a little ambush, Hambone?"

"Oh, you sweet-talking thing," Ham said.

Tag knew that he had a world of problems to solve, if he was going to pull this one off. Strategically and tactically, he knew what he needed to do, and the intelligence he needed to do it was shaping up, but there was a real question about coordination and communication, command and control. Hangay and his boys gave him part of the answer.

Tag called in Titz, Tambur, and Hangay and went over his plan with them. Hangay assured Tag that he and his boys could do it. After each of them had repeated back several times the verbal orders he was carrying to the patrols, the Mongols hit their saddles and sprinted off across the frozen Gobi. Then, Tag alerted the patrols by radio to be on the lookout for the riders.

"Are you going to tell anyone else what our battle plan might be?" Giesla asked him.

Now that things were set in motion, Tag felt events slowing to normal—to his own manic pace, that is—

and could relax enough to smile and say, "It's a piece of cake, Gies. Any two Terrapins are more than a match for a hundred men in the open, and even the guys on horses can slow them down. Tomorrow morning, just at dawn, we hit every one of the Chinese units at once. Our patrols keep them pinned down, while our strike force here moves from pocket to pocket and takes them out."

Giesla nodded, and Ham said, "I love your evil mind, Bossman."

And Fruits Tutti said, "Does dat mean I get to sleep tonight?"

"Sure does," Tag said, "and a hell of a lot warmer than those guys out there on foot."

Tag stayed up late monitoring the radio, until he was certain that Hangay and his riders had made contact with every patrol unit, then dragged his bedroll inside the living quarters, where he slept alone and only fitfully until assembly at 0400.

The two Terps that he had dispatched the previous day were already in position when Tag arrived with the strike force at 0530. The Chinese had hunkered down for the night in a stony waste strewn with boulders. With no high ground within a thousand meters, the Terrapins had moved up the depression of a water course and stationed themselves less than five hundred meters from the ChiCom camp. Tag sent four of the Terrapins from the strike force to occupy the rise to the south, which was still within easy range of 105mm guns, and lay the remaining Terps and the No Slack Too in position in the runoff bed.

Half the sun was above the horizon when Tag got word from the Terrapins on the high ground that they had the Chinese camp in their sights. He gave them the order to fire.

The Chinese were saddled up and facing into the sun when the first salvo ripped through their ranks, killing or wounding nearly a third of their number at once. Tag gave them two minutes and a second salvo from the four Terps before he sprang the rest of the trap. He ordered the four on the rise to cease fire, and led the charge out of the water course.

With two Terrapins falling away on either flank, the No Slack Too sprang into the flat, accelerating at breakneck speed under Giesla's hands. Tag rode in the open turret hatch, directing the attack from behind the naval-mounted .223 minigun. Speed, surprise, and confusion all conspired in his favor, and the No Slack Too was within three hundred meters of the Chinese before they realized they were being hit from the rear. Tag gave the order to open fire, and the carnage was brief, savage, and complete.

Four 105s echoed the roar of the XM-F4's big gun, and five Phalanx chain guns unleashed a swarm of depleted-uranium slugs among the rocks, shattering boulders with an ear-splitting din. Men broke and ran, only to be cut down by the stream of fire from Tag's turret position. The four Terrapins on the rise closed in from the south.

Taking prisoners had not been part of Tag's original plan, and it was just as well, for the Mongols were not of a mind to give quarter. Before Tag realized it, Mongols were out of their machines and moving among the wounded with small arms, adding more martyrs to the revolution. Then it was over before he could tell Tambur to order the men back to their vehicles.

Tag moved back into his commander's chair, and Ham took his place briefly in the turret. It did not take him long to get an eyeful.

Ham flopped back in his gunner's position and said, "Shee-it. I'm glad those dudes are on our side. You suppose they take scalps?"

"Used to" Titz piped in, "when we already had too many heads to carry. Government's been trying to discourage it, though."

"We've got no time to be counting coup," said Tag. "You have our next stop plotted, Gies?"

"Ready," she replied.

Tag keyed the TacNet and said, "Iron Horse, this is Butcher Boy. All follow me."

"Robber," Tambur replied.

Four hours' march for men on foot was a matter of minutes for the Terrapins and the No Slack Too, and when they fell on the rear of the next Chinese unit, which was fighting off the pesky sniper fire from Hangay and the pony patrol, they were in the middle of the formation before the Chinese's distraction could turn to terror. Even so, the column was strung out enough that one group of three men managed to break away on the point, clumping clumsily in their snowshoes as they made for the scanty protection of a low tor.

Tag was occupied on the minigun with supressing fire, giving Ham and Fruits time to reload beehive cannisters for close encounters of the worst kind for infantry. But he saw in snatches as he shifted his muzzle the figure of a rider sweeping out of the distance, saw the red of the saddle and the dull glint of a gun. Hangay. The turret spun on Tag's target, and he thought, *The damn old fool*.

Tag whipped around in the hatch, bracing his back against the rim, and pulled the minigun to eye level. He got the three men in the aperture where the cross hairs met, heard the crack of a rifle, and one of the men went down. He looked up from the sights and saw Hangay riding bolt upright in the stirrups, working the action of the Mauser at full gallop. Tag snapped back on target and tore off a burst. A second Chinese arched his back and stiffened, the stream of bullets holding him up, spinning him in a tempest of his own blood.

The third Chinese hit the ground and gamely tried to return Tag's fire. Tag found him, drew a bead, but had to slack off the trigger as Hangay flashed into the sight picture, twisting in the stirrups and shooting on the run. He worked the bolt again, fired, and steered the pony with his knees, closing in on the prone Chinese.

Except for the sporadic crack of small arms dispatches from the Mongols at the other end of the battle scene, near the rear of the column, all fell quiet. Tag eyed the bodies around him for movement as Hangay rode toward the tank at a jarring canter, the bit stretched deep in the jaws of his pony, whose eyes rolled madly.

"Titz," Tag shouted into the turret, "get your ass up here."

The translator squeezed past Tag and sat on the lip of the hatch, his feet dangling through it. He looked over the scene of battle's aftermath and said, "You are the real deal, for sure, honcho."

"Yeah," Tag said, "well, ask Hangay here what the hell his deal was. I goddam near shot him."

Hangay reined the frothing pony to a halt, causing it to rear, and shook his Mauser above his head, giving out a war cry that made Tag's scrotum tighten. The Mongol had a look in his eye that Tag had seen before only in the eyes of Indians when they got mad enough to fight. It was not hard to see this race as the ancestor of the Sioux and Cheyenne.

Titz shouted his question, listened to Hangay's oratorical answer—delivered standing from the nervous, twisting pony—and said to Tag, "Nothing to it. He wasn't going to let those three double back and surround his leader."

"Wasn't going to . . ." Tag spluttered to keep from laughing, coughed hard to cover it up, and turned away to wipe the tears from his eyes.

". . . let them surround me?" he croaked. "Titz, ask that man to remember me kindly, when the Mongols take over the world. Tell him I want to shake his hand."

Tag climbed down onto the rear deck and shook hands with Hangay.

The two Terrapins at Tag's next planned objective reported that they didn't need him; their target had been eliminated. So, after sending Yeshev a situation report—to which the Russian replied with a terse "received"—Tag turned the strike force south, leaving orders for the Terrapins and the horse soldiers in that quarter to regroup and sweep the wake of the strike force for stragglers or stray patrols.

The armored wedge drove through the Gobi, leaving behind a line in the snow, marking it plainly: "This is ours." Inside thirty minutes, they were again within sound of the guns.

One of the Chinese units that had been under hit-and-run attack from a pony patrol had managed to fight its way through to a companion unit trying to hold off a pair of Terrapins, then unlimber antitank weapons in a fissure ditch and keep the Mongols at bay. Tag surveyed the situation through binoculars from his perch on a flat-topped *ao bao* nearly a kilometer away.

"Fruits," he called to the loader, who stood in the turret of the tank below, "did you have any CS in the magazine?"

"Two rounds," Fruits said, "but they ain't on da carousel."

"How about smoke?"

"Ditto. Two rounds, Captain."

Tag knew that none of the Terrapins carried CS gas or smoke rounds, but maybe he could stretch what he had. And whatever he did, it needed to be fast. This wasn't the last of the Chinese he had to deal with. He eased off the ice-glazed stones of the *ao bao* and dropped onto the No Slack Too.

"Ham," he shouted through the turret hatch, "you think the Terp gunners are up for some indirect fire?"

"Hey, Boss, I trained 'em," Ham replied. "You let me give 'em a willy-peter for a heat lock, and they'll tear it up."

"Okay," said Tag, swinging down through the turret and into his seat, "here's the deal, then. We hammer that gully with high-angle HE, followed up with our two CS and two smoke rounds. Then, we rush them."

Tag looked up over his shoulder and said, "Titz, let Fruits put you on the radio to Tambur. You'll be coordinating the fire through Ham. And tell Tambur that if these guys want to give up, we *will* take prisoners."

The bombardment began ten minutes later, with Ham first bracketing the narrow fissure with high explosives, then splitting its banks with a white-phosphorous round. From eight-hundred, a thousand, twelve-hundred meters away, the gunners in the Terrapins that ringed the Chinese locked their target sensors on the intense heat from the WP, cross-checked their computer solutions, and at Ham's command, began firing in continuous volley. After the third round, Tag called a cease-fire to see what might crawl out of the ditch.

Nothing.

"Okay," he said, "Fruits, load the smoke first. Ham, put 'em about a third of the way in from each end, then come back with the gas in the gaps."

The badly hammered Chinese hardly reacted to the soft pop and hiss of the smoke cannisters, so stunned were they by the deadly high-explosive barrage. But when the gas rounds whistled in and men began to gag, panic raced like prairie fire up and down the ditch. Men running from the smoke hit the gas, and men fleeing the gas ran anywhere, anywhere out of the low places where it sank.

As Tag's armored noose closed on the Chinese, he saw soldiers running from the ravaged ravine unarmed, waving their hands in surrender, many falling to their knees and packing their burning faces with dirty snow.

It took twenty minutes for the smoke to clear, and another twenty to sort the wounded from the dead in the ditch. The two Terrapins and the cavalry riding drag came into sight, enough muscle to handle more than eighty prisoners, freeing Tag to move to the next ambush.

It was shaping up to be a big day.

9

Death worked overtime that afternoon and evening. Tag and his reaction force struck three more times before dark, then spent much of the night directing the movement of prisoners and policing the scattered battle scenes. A stray patrol caused some casualties among one squadron of mounted troops, but paid for it with their lives. Tag did not pursue the report that some of the Mongols rode from the scene with bulging sacks hung from their pommels. It was dawn of the next day before they made contact with the column of tanks and trucks that Yeshev dispatched to pick up the prisoners, who numbered more than three hundred, all that remained of the crack battalion of Chinese winter rangers. It grieved the Mongols that they could not bury the other hundreds of dead Chinese and deny them the honor of a sky burial, when their corpses thawed and the vultures returned in the spring.

Tag awoke from dozing in his seat, blinked at the sunlight falling on his face through the open hatch, then leaned forward and stood in it. Giesla was juking them through the zigzag path between the mines and razor wire of the bivouac perimeter. Throughout the Mongol sector of the compound, open fires were burning. Battle flags and national banners snapped from the shafts of lances and lariat poles stuck in the snow. A dozen or more ponies were already tethered outside the yurts, and there was some brisk movement going on around the fires. Tag caught a whiff of roasting meat.

He dropped himself off at the operations tent and sent Giesla and the guys to service the No Slack Too and get themselves some rest, then went inside to make his report to Yeshev and compose a transmission for Menefee.

"Thanks for the backup," he said to Minski, who had greeted him as he came in.

"Really, Captain," Minski said, his fussy good humor not nicked by sarcasm, "you would have been offended if we had come. That would have been nice. Unfortunately, command would also have been offended. I'll show you why when you have finished your report, unless you want to bathe first."

"Bathe?" said Tag. "You are a real hoot, Major."

"No, no," said Minski, "I am serious. The Mongols have been melting snow and heating water in preparation for you. They have planned what I think must be a very special fete, one worthy of a bath."

These crazy fuckers, Tag thought, get in more partying in a combat zone than I can on furlough. But he just shook his head wearily and sat down at a message desk to work on his report to Menefee until Yeshev arrived.

He had it done in an hour, and what he then learned from Minski and Yeshev stirred his concern. The bottom line was that in the process of collating all the intelligence gathered during the recent days of fighting, G-2 had realized that the actual engagements did not reflect the level of activity in and around the likely staging areas. It was command's conclusion that none of the assaults so far represented the major push they expected. With the weather cleared and holding good, aerial observation and satellite reconnaissance had both been stepped up, but there was an ominous dearth of detectable activity on the Chinese side. For at least the next forty-eight to seventy-two hours, only security patrols would leave the bivouac.

Tag grunted. "Sounds like command and the Chinese are waiting to see who blinks first."

"Very likely," said Yeshev. "Also, there is the weather. The Chinese forays so far have not been helped by the weather, and they still harbor old superstitions about the north wind being inauspicious. Perhaps they are waiting for a south breeze."

"First you're skeptical about using cavalry, and now you want to call up superstitions to plot strategy?" Tag said archly.

Yeshev settled into the crude, massive wooden chair one of the men had scrounged for him, adjusted the sheepskins under his legs, and said, "The Chinese communists and the millions of Chinese who abet them are the most curious breed of political animal on the face of the earth, Captain Tag, just as China itself is a massive anomaly of culture. The structural dynamics of power have not changed significantly in China for more than twenty-five centuries. Mandarins have been replaced by Party cadres, that is all. Instead of the Yellow Emperor, they have the Red Star.

"Still, I think it is less Party dogma that determines Party policy, foreign and domestic, than it is Chinese assumptions about the world, assumptions that will always be different from yours and mine, Captain Tag."

Tag, finding Yeshev's commentary fascinating, rose, poured himself another cup of dark tea, and asked the Russian to go on.

"Chinese thought, and so the Chinese mind, is often more subtle than supple. This is the Confucian influence, with its emphasis on propriety and order and duties of station. It is this line of thought that has gained hegemony in China, overwhelming Taoism or Buddhism as the dominant chord in political and social development, although resonances of these others do remain. Astrology is still widely practiced, Buddhist holidays are still celebrated, and military commanders will still consult ancient geomancers' charts before establishing positions. So, do not think it crackpot to imagine that they may be waiting for a favorable wind."

"Sounds to me like you've read more than just Sun Tzu," Tag said, referring to the author of the Chinese classic *Art of War*.

"I spent nearly a year at our mission in Beijing in the nineties, and I have not stopped studying them since. Anytime you have questions about the Chinese, please ask me, Captain. I have opinions about almost everything."

Tag acknowledged the pleasantry with a smile, and said, "Thanks, Colonel. I'd like to do that some time. Right now, though, I think I'll check on my crew and see about that bath the major mentioned."

The activity around the Mongol compound reminded Tag of field day on a battleship. Every man there seemed to be simultaneously tending at least three jobs—policing the area of trash and horse droppings, carrying cooking pots and whole, skinned sheep to the fires, plaiting beads and conchos into the ponies' manes and tails, brushing out coats of dyed and embroidered wool, standing naked in the snow and pouring basins of water over their heads, tuning musical instruments, spreading fresh straw, and, indeed, feeding clean snow into two steaming cauldrons of bath water.

Tag made his way through the throng, exchanging back slaps with the Terrapin crews and accepting a bottle of midmorning beer, until he reached the No Slack Too, where Ham and Fruits—scrubbed, shaven, and in fresh uniforms—stood sentinel while Giesla bathed behind a screen of ponchos strung from lariat poles. Steam roiled out of the enclosure and into the freezing air like smoke from a smoldering volcano.

Tag took a pull from the beer and passed it to Ham. "Hey," he called to Giesla, "you gonna save me some water?"

Giesla dashed water from her face and shouted, "Haul your own water, Max Tag. I do not come out until this freezes. But you may bring me a towel; this one is wet."

Fruits took the beer from Ham and said, "Aw, she's

ribbin' you, Captain Max. Dem Mongols'll bring you all da water you need."

"Yeah?" Tag said. "Well, I see you two didn't stand on ceremony."

"Orders from a superior officer, Boss," Ham said.

"That is right," said Giesla. "I did not want anyone waiting for me to finish. So, you go play soldier for a while longer, Max. And bring me that towel."

"I see what you mean," Tag said to Ham.

He fetched Giesla a towel, left the liter bottle of beer with Ham and Fruits, and wandered back out into the busy throng of Mongol soldiers, making his way in the general direction of Tambur's yurt.

Like Tag, Tambur had not yet cleaned up, but he was sprawled outside his yurt on a pallet of ammunition boxes high with rugs and skins, reclining on one elbow and waving a bottle of sweet wine as he directed the preparations going on around him. Nearby, Tag saw a horse with a familiar red felt saddle, but no sign of Hangay. Titz was seated on the edge of Tambur's dais, stripping flesh from a blackened rib bone with his yellow teeth. Tambur waved for Tag to come and sit.

Tag flopped on a pile of skins, took a drink, returned the bottle to Tambur, and said, "Don't your men want to rest, get a little sleep?"

"Rest night; sleep dead. Today we celibate," Tambur said, waving the bottle.

"Don't you dig what an occasion this is, kahuna?" Titz chimed in, his mouth full of stringy meat. "These men are gods, man. They'll be put in songs and sung about by generations, just like the great khan Ghenghis. For some of their families, this is the first victory in generations—and what a deal! Handfuls of horsemen capturing hundreds, slaying thousands—"

"Whoa," Tag said. "Thousands? There was maybe a battalion, Titz, about eight hundred men. Tops."

"Don't confuse the issue," said Titz. "This is their page in our history; let them write it to suit. Okay?"

"Tens of thousands," Tag said.

"Ten T'ousman Victimy," Tambur bellowed. "*Gar*."

"Gar!" shouted Titz and every other Mongol in hearing.

Tag had a trick of yowling like a cougar, and he did it now, leaping up into a crouch, throwing back his head, and letting the open, throaty moan well out of his chest, ending with a whoop.

"Titz," he said, "where's the beer?"

Tag swung back by the No Slack Too, carrying three bottles of beer in a helmet he held by the strap and drinking from a bottle in his hand. Ham and Fruits were still loitering around the tank, while Giesla dressed inside the yurt, so Tag stripped and stood in the washtub and poured basins of hot water over himself, punctuated by long pulls from the bottle of faintly apple-scented beer, scrubbed down with GI soap, doused himself with more water, then called for another beer so he could do it all over again.

When he was through, Tag wrapped himself in a towel and picked up his dirty clothes. Hurrying out of the cold toward the yurt, he stopped in his tracks as Giesla emerged from behind the flaps. She had changed into Mongol costume, and she was stunning. The voluminous legs of her nip-waisted white woolen culotte skirt were stuffed into the tops of high black boots, and her body was wrapped in a short fur-trimmed felt jacket, its panels dyed in bright, geometric primaries. On her head she wore, set at a rakish angle, a round flat-crowned hat, like the kind cowboys call a "Winchester." Her ash-blond hair fell free from beneath its brim.

"Good goddam," said Tag, his jaw falling slack. He felt utterly ridiculous standing there shivering up a mess of goose bumps and holding a soggy towel in one hand and a wad of laundry in the other. But he couldn't do much else for the moment, except watch Giesla tug out the wrinkles in her costume and take a slow, model's turn in front of the yurt.

"Do you like it?" she said, admiring the drape of the culottes across her thigh.

"It's . . . it's killer," Tag stammered. "Where did you . . .?"

"Oh, Titz found it for me somewhere," she said. Then, looking up as though she were seeing Tag for the first time, Giesla broke into a laugh.

"Max," she said, stifling a giggle, "just look at you."

"Oh, bullshit," said Tag. He whipped the towel from his waist, threw it over one shoulder, and stalked into the yurt with all the dignity he could muster, the muscular white moons of his ass last to slide behind the flaps.

Everyone had gone from his vicinity when Tag came back out, dressed now in a fresh jumpsuit topped with a parka liner, so he had to wend his way alone through the thickening crowd, which now included several Russians as well, until he found Giesla, Ham, Fruits, and Yeshev all lolling on Tambur's dais, drinking wine and beer and watching the barbecue turn on the fire, while a young soldier in a dramatic pose, one leg braced on the ammo boxes, sang to the sounds drawn from a two-string fiddle by another soldier sitting at his feet.

Old Hangay elbowed his way out of the crowd and over to Tag's side, where he shouted something and pressed a bottle into his hand. Tag glanced at it, saw the initials VSOP and the word "cognac," took a cautious sip, and passed it back. Hangay waved his hands palms-out in refusal.

"That's yours, big honcho," Titz said in Tag's ear. "He says you're his khan now. He's thanking you for leading him into battle. That good stuff, it's just for you."

"Okay. Okay," Tag said. "Thank him, but tell him that in my horde, we all share alike." He held out the bottle while Titz translated.

Hangay smiled and bobbed his head and held up his

thumb and first finger a half-inch apart. Then he took the bottle and drank off three inches.

Tag took the bottle back and goggled at the air at the top, feeling a little resentful at the way Hangay treated Old Pale cognac.

Tag carried the bottle over to the dais, elbowed Ham aside, and scooted up next to Giesla, who had thrown a blue-and-white figured rug over her.

"Cognac before lunch seems to be the custom here," he said.

Giesla turned her tired, happy eyes on him and said, "Lunch? Did I miss breakfast? Can I have somebody flogged for that?"

"I'll hand you the varlet's head," said Tag, "just point him out to me."

"I think," she said, taking the bottle from him and drawing the cork, "that I am going to like being the consort of the khan of a great horde."

She passed the bottle over Tag to Ham, who took it and said, "That's fine, just don't be gettin' any ideas about consorts havin' any eunuchs, lady."

"What's on the musical program?" Tag asked.

"Oh, this," said Giesla, her voice brightening as she rose on her elbow, "this is the song competition, Max, about our battles, the victory of your horde. Each of these men"— she nodded toward the queue of soldiers standing to one side of the dais—"will sing his song of the 'Victory of Ten Thousand,' and Tambur will choose the best five to compete before you."

"And I choose the winner?"

"That is right. Then, that man's song will become the song every other man will incorporate into his family song line."

"What's a 'song line'?" Tag asked, taking the bottle back from Ham.

"It is a family history and a family epic, all the tall tales about your grandfathers who cut down the Sahara forest to make the Sahara desert put up to memory in songs. There are national song lines, too, I gather, the sagas of the great khans and the great movements of the people and, especially, about when they ruled China. There are even scraps of song memory about Europe, references to fighting the *Keltas* and the *Poleskas*. Titz has been a great help."

Mild fatigue buoyed by excitement, a bath, and a couple of ounces of old cognac left Tag content enough to survive fully ten minutes of the musical audition, but in the end he had to despair of ever developing an ear for Mongol melodies. He knew he'd get his fill judging the finals. But no sooner had he stretched and said he wanted to circulate than Yeshev, Giesla, Ham, and Fruits were all on their feet as well, and so his casual stroll turned into an inspection tour, and he felt more than ever like a tourist on some exotic, foreign midway.

Out in the fields of fire between the tank perimeter and the wire, a variation of Mongol polo was going on, in which something small and furry was picked up on lance point from the ground, held aloft and ridden with a while, then tossed to a comrade when other riders closed in. It was a furious game, played with sharpened cattle prods and very lustily. Tag saw blood on the legs of more than one horse and rider, but he did not get close enough to see what the thing of hair was that they chased.

Sidling back toward the heart of the throng, the group passed the wrestlers preparing for their matches. The men were laughing with one another, affixing bells and metal studs to their vests, and they all turned to Tag to hail him with shouts of "Gar!" and "Ten T'ousman Victimy." Tag wondered what sort of wickedness Tambur's pidgin had worked on two languages.

Arriving again at Tambur's divan, Tag saw that the first of the sheep were coming off the fires and being dismembered on a hasty trestle of boxes. There were pots of saffron rice, transparent noodles, bowls of tough Russian beans, and some sort of spicy pickled vegetable with whole cloves of garlic swimming in the brine. Trays and platters of all these were placed upon the dais, along with more beer and wine and one bottle of pepper vodka that Yeshev had supplied, and Westerners and Mongols alike fell on the feast with a will, with the incessant soughing of a two-string fiddle for accompaniment. Tag found the sound, if not soothing, at least less intrusive than when joined by a voice. They ate, belched, grinned inanely, and threw the bones back into the fire, where one of them exploded, causing a ripple of relieved laughter among those who had not hit the ground.

While soldiers were clearing the trays and empty bottles, and others were spreading fresh straw in front of the dais, Hangay came up and spoke to Titz, who spoke to Tambur before turning to Tag and saying, "Hangay wants his daughter-in-law to do a dance for you, kahuna. He says he's sorry she's not a Mongol—she's from Xinjiang, a Moslem, you know—but he says she is graceful enough to dance for a khan."

"Good enough for me," Tag said. "Bring on the dancing girls."

Tag remembered the young woman from the compound and had noted at the time that she looked different from the others there—taller, with a longer face and rounder eyes. She was dressed in her nomadic best, though barefooted, her wrists and ankles tinkling with bracelets of silver and brass, a heavy choker of silver, turquoise, and coral around her long neck, and huge earrings swaying from her ears. She did not look at the dais but communicated briefly with the fiddle player, who struck up a rhythmic run of quarter tones. The woman added the clack of small finger cymbals and commenced to dance.

The dance began at her feet, with slow movements that barely stirred the straw beneath them. Then her hips began to undulate, then her back and arms. At last she was in full, sensual motion, passing through postures that reminded Tag at times of the profile paintings in Egyptian tombs and at others of sweeping designs he had seen in the Mogul paintings from northern India. Even here in this wild and antique land, she was an exotic, a living token and reminder of history and the geopolitics of conquest. There was an abandon in her movements that was also somehow remote, just the opposite of what Americans euphemistically call exotic dance. She used a scarf for emphasis, but this was no striptease. Her face was radiant as a virgin's, transported by the dance that she had become.

When she was done, she stopped all at once and simply walked away. Tag led the applause.

As it died down, Tag heard the fiddle player running playfully through a jig-time version of "Red River Valley," and Giesla, lounging beside him on the rugs, said, "Good. Now I will sing for the khan."

She stood and stepped to the edge of the dais, motioned for the fiddler to slow his tempo, then sang the song in German, in a full alto voice that gave timbre and depth to a tune that Tag, through long familiarity, had resigned to the slag heap of sentimentality. Perhaps, he thought, it was fatigue and cognac, but he found himself moved by the song, faintly homesick, choked with emotion.

Giesla rejoined him beneath the rug they shared, nodding modestly in response to the applause and cheers, and drank from a lidded cup of hot tea and cognac.

"Max," she said, "I cannot remember enjoying a day so much since we left your parents' ranch. But will it last much longer? I am suddenly very tired."

"You can probably bow out any time," he said, "but I have to at least stay for the singing. Struggle through it with me, if you can."

She squeezed his leg beneath the rug and said, "Always."

The paeans to the "Ten T'ousman Victimy" were blessedly brief, and Tag was a little drunk by this time, so he managed to muster a show of enthusiasm. One of the songs did stand out to him for its rolling cadence and sudden changes in register, from bass to falsetto. To his surprise, Tambur's glance also registered approval, and the crowd generally ratified Tag's choosing that tune the winner, although he had to sit through it again as a result.

The young women and girls from Hangay's brood coaxed Ham and Fruits and two of the Russian tankers into the social dancing that followed, and Tag and Giesla took the opportunity to slip away back to the yurt.

Tag stoked the stove, and Giesla pulled piles of bedding off the cots to make them a pallet on the floor. Soon they were snug under the covers, sharing a cup of tea spiked with the last of the cognac.

"Drunk and in bed before dark—what decadence!" Giesla exclaimed. "I think becoming a great khan has ruined you, Max."

"Silence, consort," he said. "And come here and consort with me."

"Duty, duty," Giesla sighed as she slid her leg between his.

Tag awoke the next morning more embarrassed than hungover: he and Giesla were still curled on the floor, while Ham and Fruits were asleep in their beds, and a sly, grinning Mongol private was feeding rough lumps of coal into the stove at the foot of the pallet. Tag waved him out, dressed without waking the others, and stumbled off to find some strong tea before he checked in at the operations tent.

Not everyone on the Mongolian front had had a party the previous day. There had been more than a dozen probes and incursions along the line, even one missile attack, although the fighters that scrambled could not locate the launcher. Satellite reconnaissance had detected some vehicular movement during the night, but live flyovers had not been able to confirm it, either. Command was getting increasingly

concerned that the Chinese were trying to draw out the
defenders and engage them in the open, something command was not ready to do. At the same time, there was a
concern that failure to contest the Chinese positions might
give them time to concentrate enough troops to overrun the
lines. It was a dilemma made worse by the competition for
control that was shaping up within the shaky infrastructure
of Mongol, Russian, and NATO brigades, a contest made
clear to Tag by the communication he received that morning
from Menefee.

In it, Satin Ass restated that Tag's orders came only from
him, Menefee, or from him through Yeshev. Any orders
Yeshev followed or passed along had to come from the
headquarters unit Menefee was attached to, or Tag was to
ignore them. Tag had only in the past few days begun to
feel he and Yeshev had the kind of relationship that would
grow stronger with exercise, and the hints in Menefee's
message felt like the thin edge of a wedge being driven
between them. He decided to show it to the Russian and
tell him what he thought.

Yeshev drummed his fingers on the arm of his rough
wooden chair, looking as dark and brooding as a character
from a Russian novel. As one who had had to swim his
entire military life through the riptides and crosscurrents
of politics, Yeshev was only too familiar with the possible
repercussions of gossip, innuendo, and mistrust, how they
can rip the confidence that must exist between commanders and gut the morale of the troops. That, along with
the blunderings of the general staff, had sealed the fate
of the First Guards Tank Army in Germany, leading to
Tag's almost single-handed defeat of it. Yeshev was not
willing to see that repeated, especially in the very presence
of his victor, whom he had come to respect as an ally and,
hedgingly, to regard as a friend.

"Max," Yeshev said at last, surprising Tag with the use
of his given name, "I think we both know what we need

to do, regardless of command. Still, I do feel bound to keep the main body of this regiment—perhaps *battalion*, I should say—to keep it intact as a fighting unit. With that said, we—you and I—will do what is necessary."

"Colonel, . . ."

"Feyodr, Max. In private, we will not stand on rank."

"Feyodr," Tag continued, "command may have put itself on hold, but we still have patrols to run. Right?"

"Correct."

"But we don't have any specific orders about number, size, or range, do we?"

Yeshev smiled. "Go on, Max," he said.

"In addition to the armor, this outfit is carrying nearly a hundred wheeled vehicles, most of them with mounted light machine guns, and there are at least a dozen heavy machine guns we don't need on the perimeter. You let me play with the hardware and give me enough men to handle it, and I can double, triple, our patrol strength, and provide enough firepower to give ground troops the fits."

Yeshev rose heavily and walked to the stove. "You have forty-eight hours," he said, pouring himself more tea. "I will get the additional fuel here by then."

"That's a promise?" Tag said.

"Only to see that you make yours good," said Yeshev. "Only that." He kept his grin turned toward the wall.

10

The satellite and aerial intelligence that came in over the following two days was not entirely worthless, any more than was the data gathered by Yeshev's short-range recon patrols, but none of it gave Tag any clear idea of what they might have to face when the big push came. Heedful of his ignorance, he did everything possible to prepare for the worst.

The Chinese build-up on their side of the border—in what they called Inner Mongolia—was no secret. In fact, the Chinese seemed to be arraying troops and armor in poses for the flying cameras. But inside the border, in the areas of wasteland where the Chinese vanguard was suspected to be hiding, there was almost nothing. An occasional foot patrol, the odd probe along the line, but no hard evidence of large troop concentrations or preparations for a mass movement. Still, the suspicions were strong, and the waiting had put everyone's nerves on high alert. The troops working under Tag's direction, however, had little time or energy for nervous speculation.

Beginning the day after the celebration of the Ten T'ousman Victimy, he had assembled his and Yeshev's personal crews at dawn to begin surveying their resources, counting every piece of rolling stock and every marginally employed man and weapon in the bivouac, and before noon he had their complete list. In addition to the No Slack Too and the eighteen effective Terrapins, the Russians had conjured up a pair of BMPs in antitank configuration that were officially on the "inoperable" list but needed only some minor tinkering to be battle ready. Added to that, the men had tallied six one-ton personnel carriers, four five-ton trucks, and four all-purpose vehicles similar to the HUMV, which Tag still insisted on calling jeeps.

For armaments, seven of the vehicles already carried 7.62mm machine guns; one of the PCs was mounted with a Russian 107mm recoilless rifle; and there were seven 12.7mm heavy machine guns that could be pressed into service, as well as a full course of small arms, grenade launchers, rocket-propelled anti-armor grenades, and a couple of crew-served antitank rocket stands. Tag ordered the vehicles, weapons, and the men Yeshev had assigned to him into the shop area, where the work of refitting would be done.

The field shop that had been set up at the bivouac was surprisingly complete, lacking only an actual building. It boasted a pair of tank retrievers (which, built on tank chassis, Tag eyed covetously), a truck full of spare parts and another full of tools, including a small forge, four arc welders, and two oxyacetylene outfits. To the four Russian mechanics and four helpers, Tag added himself, his men, and two Mongol mechanics, with everyone else assigned as gofers to hump supplies and materials and keep the workmen supplied with food and hot tea.

Tag scratched a spark beneath the nozzle of his torch, and a blue spike of flame popped to life. He eyed it closely as he adjusted the valve and fed oxygen to the flame with the thumb release.

"Okay, you vultures," he said to the men, "here's our first order of business. We're going to scrounge every square inch of armor and steel plate that we can scavenge to reinforce the wheeled vehicles. Meanwhile, Giesla, get these other people to work with the arc welders, mounting the machine guns."

"Whadda we s'posed to use for mounts?" Fruits asked.

"Be creative," said Tag.

The Russian mechanics were at first reluctant to let the vehicles in their care be cannibalized, but soon got caught up in the intensity Tag brought to the work. It amazed even them how much plate could be stripped from the utilitarian bodies of the few trucks and the track skirts of the APCs that they had down for repairs. The one T-80 in the shop was off-limits, although Tag did loot it for its machine gun ammunition, swearing to the mechanics that he had okayed it with Yeshev.

When darkness fell, Tag cranked up the generator, and they worked under floods until the cold of night drove them to their tents and yurts. But they were at it again at first light.

By afternoon of the second day, Tag could stand back and behold his creation—and feel a little like Rube Goldberg. The contraptions were the ugliest assembly of raw plate and hammered armor ever hung on a chassis, every one looking like some modern sculptor's dark fantasy of an armored attack vehicle. There were sheets of runway matting, beds ripped from trucks, BMP fenders that had been torched off and forged flat, flattened grease drums and shell casings, anything that would turn a bullet, and all of it welded to hoods and doors and sides and undercarriages. Each of the jeeps was mounted with a 12.7mm, as were three of the trucks. The rest, including the PC with the 107mm, had one or two 7.62mm machine guns. Each truck and PC was crewed by a driver and four men fielding a variety of small arms and antitank weapons. The rocket stands were mounted in the rear of two of the big trucks, where they could be fired from the open tailgates.

Tag liked everything he saw, except the size of the fuel tanks. Those hogs were going to suck some juice, but he didn't see much hope of conning Yeshev out of a towed fuel cell. He'd just have to see what he could turn up in a fifty, maybe sixty mile radius.

With more than an hour of daylight left, Tag ordered the vehicles taken out for a shakedown, while he went for a confab with Yeshev.

Yeshev was pleased with Tag's report. He turned to the map pinned on the operations table—there were no strategic terrain features, so Yeshev had not had a sand table made—smoothed out the acetate overlay with the backs of his fingernails, and said, "What looks good to you?"

"Well," Tag said slyly, "I'd usually go to my superior officer for guidance in a situation like this."

"Good," said Yeshev. "Here is my guidance: do not be wrong."

"Now *that*," said Tag, "clearly came from Colonel Menefee. God, the burden of duty. Okay, you tell me if I'm right or not. What we want to know is how much of what the Chinese have where. Right?"

Yeshev nodded uncertainly.

"Okay. Now, we could stretch the Terrapins and the No Slack Too out to, say, a three-hundred-kilometer radius, but if we want to make the best use of our cavalry and the armored vehicles, we'll have to operate within, oh, seventy-five or eighty klicks, tops. To maximize that, I say we saturate this area, here."

He pointed to an area southeast of the bivouac, in the same quadrant where the initial air assault had been thwarted.

"I'm guessing that they had more stuff stashed out here somewhere, maybe just waiting to pick it up when they come back through."

"You know that there has been some activity in that quadrant?" said Yeshev.

"Good," said Tag. "All the more reason we need to go have a look."

"What will be your order of battle?"

"About like before. I'll put the jeeps out with the Terrapin and cavalry patrols and keep the heavy trucks and PCs with the strike force, save more gas that way, and let the BMPs run flank security for the strike group."

"Fine, Max, fine," said Yeshev. "Give me the rest of it before you move out in the morning."

"In the morning? So it's a go, then?"

"My guidance would be that you leave before dawn."

"And I'll ever follow wisdom," Tag said.

Before he blew out the lantern that night, Tag had met with Tambur and the newly incorporated Russians— a motley of cooks, drivers, clerks, and green conscripts— gone over the patrol plan with them, worked up a radio protocol, and made sure everybody had maps, chow, and all of the right kinds of ammunition. He went over what to do in case of air attack and what to do if they had to fall back—in a hurry.

Assembly was at 0300. The riders went out at 0330, the Terrapin pairs at 0400, and the rest of the patrol at 0415.

Because of the armored trucks, Tag's column had to move at a 40 kph crawl, so once they were out of sight of the bivouac, he extended the flanks and the point, using Terps to fill in the gaps, so they could eyeball more country as they moved. But when the morning dawned cold and still, with only a high layer of thin clouds to cut the glare, none of the elements had anything to report. The ring of high ground, where Tag and Yeshev had discovered the initial staging area, lay to the south of Tag's azimuth, but the Terrapin patrol in that sector reported no signs of fresh movement there. Tag scanned his maps again, searching for any similar, subtle pieces of topography that the Chinese might have used. But at 0800, one of the prowling jeeps found it for him.

The report came in of approximately fifty troops in

defensive formation along the line of a rise above a water course, less than ten kilometers from Tag's own location. He quickly diverted a pair of Terrapins toward the site, notified the other units of the contact, and turned the strike force in that direction.

Tag swept the near flank of the Chinese position at a distance of more than a kilometer, halted the strike force, and went forward himself on foot to reconnoiter.

Dmitri Tsarpov, the gunner from Yeshev's crew, was in the jeep that made the initial sighting, and he led Tag in a low crawl through the crusty snow to a vantage point less than three hundred meters from the water course. Tag brought out his binoculars and settled his elbow in the snow.

It was difficult at first for him to distinguish the Chinese fighting positions on the lip of the rise. They were well concealed and not thrown up recently. But even after several minutes, he could count no more than two dozen two-man bunkers. Scouring the slope behind them that ran down to the water course, he thought he could make out irregularities in the snowbank, but little else.

Tag edged backward below the low crest and said to Dmitri, "Well, good work, but it looks like we'll have to go in. Keep that thin-skin out of the way, though, when the shooting starts. Let the Terrapins handle this."

"My pleasure," said Dmitri, evincing a tanker's aversion to exposing himself to direct small-arms fire.

There was nothing exotic about Tag's plan to take the Chinese position. It was quick and dirty, relying entirely on firepower. Two Terrapins, one on either flank of the Chinese, would lay down suppressing fire, while the other four and the No Slack Too knocked out the bunkers one by one with cannons.

"Oh, yes," Ham Jefferson said, "the old pin-'em-down-and-blow-'em-up strategy. Very creative, Bossman."

"It's that or send you out there with a knife and grenade," said Tag.

"I appreciate it," Ham said, "but I'd as soon ride."

"Load aitch-ee," said Tag.

The fire from the two Terrapins fell obliquely on the flanks of the Chinese position, leaving the defenders unprepared for the barrage that opened up from their rear. Breaking into the open all abreast, the No Slack Too and the remaining six Terrapins launched their first salvo on the run, then scattered into what fighting positions they could find to continue their methodical bombardment.

Shooting from more than three hundred meters and having to rely solely on their optical sights, the gunners were not setting any rapid-fire records, but were steadily blasting breaches in the breastworks of rammed snow, when they began receiving counter fire from antitank weapons.

There was one, and then there were a half-dozen thick, white contrails webbing the air between the Terrapins and the Chinese, contrails left by the *Yu Ying*, or Cormorant, developed by the Chinese after the American Dragon system and a dangerous weapon against most armor. Tag recognized them at once, especially by the ferocity of their explosions.

"Hard cover. All units, this is Butcher Boy. Take hard cover."

As Giesla threw the No Slack Too into reverse, a Cormorant kissed the turret just inboard of the gun mantle, and the impetus lent by its detonation to the momentum Giesla had begun smashed the XM-F4 backward. Titz, unbelted, flew through the turret; Tag jammed a finger against his console; and Fruits took an elbow in the belly while trying to grab the tumbling Titz.

"Holy shit," Ham said, "this is some serious kimchi, Boss."

Tag pulled hard on his finger, felt it pop, and a thin sweat broke out on his brow. "Yeah," he said. "It's gonna take a little longer than I thought."

Tag put out the word to the Terps to fight from cover and use their Phalanx systems if they had to, to keep the Chinese honest.

"Shoot and scoot, Max?" Giesla asked.

"You're beginning to talk like a tanker," he said. "Find us a place to fight from."

As Giesla maneuvered them to a new position, Tag ran a radio check and found one of the Terrapins not responding.

Giesla locked one track and spun them in behind a low hummock that covered little besides the glacis of the tank, and Tag said through the intercom, "Gunner's choice. Fruits, man the Phalanx."

Refocusing his scope on the bunkered bank, Tag saw the positions being gnawed by Phalanx fire and spat out of the ground by HE detonations. The No Slack Too shuddered under the rolling recoil of its own 37mm chain gun, rocked hard back on its carriage with the report from the main tube, and then was moving again in evasive sprints, as Giesla searched for their next position.

She took them forward, ploughed through a deep, crusty drift, and gained them a short crest on its other side. Ham got off two shots in quick order, as Fruits dusted up the shelled bunkers with the Phalanx, and then Tag called a cease-fire and called up the trucks and PCs.

The Terrapin that Tag had lost radio contact with had taken a hit that knocked out its communications, but it was still fit to fight. He dispatched six men from the trucks to accompany two Terrapins to sweep the position, leaving the two Terrapins on the flanks and the two BMP outriders in place for local security. Meanwhile, he wanted to see what it was these guys had been protecting.

On the approach to the water course from Tag's side, there was no definition to the bed. In wet weather, it was as broad as it had to be. The far bank, however, where the Chinese had set their emplacements, was an imposing height, fully ten feet above the floor of the depression and commanding all the ground to the north. But it was here, on the face of the bank, that Tag had set his sights, for something about the way the snow lay at no natural angle of repose told him that this was the payoff.

When he got the all-clear signal from the men on the bank, Tag ordered them down to inspect the face, then got out himself to supervise. The face was frozen, glazed with melt-ice, and the men had to break out track stretchers from the Terrapins' tool boxes to open the surface. One of the Russians gave a shout, and Tag went to see what he had found, which was bamboo. Three feet into a washtub-size hole in the frozen snow, there were two bamboo poles the size of Tag's wrist, lashed at right angles with stiff wire and covered in coarse bamboo matting.

"Get a couple of those trucks over here," Tag shouted to Titz, who was hobbling around outside the No Slack Too, rubbing various parts of himself. "Get some winches in here. You," he said, gesturing to the Russian who had made the hole, "make it bigger."

Two of the five-ton trucks growled up to the bank, paid out cable from their winches for the men to hook on the bamboo, then locked their brakes and began hauling in. Ice and bamboo squealed in protest, cracked, and shattered, as a section of the bank the size of a wall peeled loose, exposing the dugout cavern just high enough for Liberation Lorries mounted with missile stands to park, and just deep enough for the tracked launchers of ground-attack Silk Worms. Tag could see at least one of each.

"Okay," he shouted, "let's get everybody in here. Let's take this son of a bitch down."

Men and machines swarmed into the runoff bed and began ripping with track stretchers and winch hooks at the false face of the bank, exposing two hundred meters of bunker in less than an hour.

The arsenal that the bank had hidden was formidable, so much so that Tag was stunned when he looked at the preliminary tally. All told, there were ten Liberation Lorries tricked out as multiple-launch rocket vehicles, and twenty-five of the more sophisticated Silk Worm launchers. The Silk Worm was an old system, developed in the eighties as a naval cruise missile, but the Chinese had modified it and kept it in their arsenal as a very effective medium-range ground-attack missile. Each of the low-slung tracked launchers had two rails, and each of the lorries six tubes. The multiple launchers were armed, and there were missile bodies on the launch rails of the mobile stands, but no warheads. These were stacked in an ammo dump at one end of the bunker.

When Tag heard this, he mounted the fender of the No Slack Too and told Giesla to drive to the far end of the bunker. The last scraps of the bamboo facade were still coming down, and men were still milling around to ogle the captured hardware, when the air-alarm klaxon blared inside the No Slack Too.

"Incoming aircraft," Tag bellowed. "Take cover."

He scrambled across the glacis and dropped through the hatch into his commander's seat.

"Where are they?" he said, strapping the CVC to his chin and hitting the keys on his console.

"Coming from zero nine hundred, hot and low, Boss. Six blips," said Ham. "Holy shit, we got launch, multiple launch."

Tag armed the Phalanx for robotic radar response, and it came instantly to life, spraying skeins of depleted uranium slugs at the incoming missiles, the closed-loop radar shrinking the cones of fire, throwing blizzards of bullets in the missiles' paths, while he locked the War Clubs on the planes themselves and sent four of the needle-nose MiG-busters sizzling out of the farings.

Explosions went up all around them, near enough to jolt the thirty-ton XM-F4, and 20mm cannon fire raked the men caught in the open. Tag's single Phalanx had knocked out four of the oncoming missiles—four of twelve—and two of the War Clubs scored hits on the MiG-27s, vaporizing one in the eruption of its own fuel and sending the other to the desert floor in flaming cartwheels. The remaining four made it through and delivered their first stick of ordnance. Eight five-hundred-pound bombs thundered into the water course, one of them landing between a five-ton truck and one of the PCs, sending both vehicles flying like broken toys. The air itself was stunned by the explosions, and men screamed in ripped-gut pain.

Tag yelled over the No Slack Too's exterior speaker, "Get to your vehicles and disperse. Air evasive tactics. Use your chain guns. Get in your vehicles.

"Giesla," he said, turning to look at her, "get us the hell out of this bowl."

Blips lit the edge of the radar screen again, and Ham said, "I got 'em coming back."

"Roger," Tag said. He had only four War Clubs left in the racks, and he had to pick his moment to use them. If he launched from too far away, the MiGs would have time to take defensive measures, deploy flares and confetti and radar decoys. If he waited too long, they would already be using those measures to cover their approach to their target. There was a narrow window in there, and Tag was gambling on making it through.

"Lock on bogeys one and four," Tag said.

"Lock confirmed," Ham replied.

A War Club screamed from either side of the turret, and Tag said, "Shot away."

He took shallow breaths and watched the radar screen. The launch program he had used for this pair of missiles would keep them skimming the ground for a long way before they blasted upward in a high-angle attack intended to foil both forward- and backward-looking radar. It was a program designed to take out the elusive Russian Havoc helicopters, never meant for use against MiGs.

The two MiGs went up almost simultaneously, and their pilots never knew what hit them. One moment they were lining up the water course in their bomb sights, and the next they were blown into unconsciousness by twenty kilos of TNT exploding through the bellies of their planes. Both aircraft careened in sickening spins to the desert floor, exploding in red-black infernos.

The remaining pair of streaking MiGs released another round of heat-seeking missiles and a volley of rockets, then opened up with their cannons, but by now the vehicles were scattering, and the Terrapin crews had brought their Phalanx guns to bear. Most of the smaller rockets survived the hail of bullets from the chain guns, but one of the MiGs did not. Its engine flamed out as it banked away, the plane shuddering against the sky. A scarf of dark smoke waved from its vent, then the MiG slipped off the air and into a crash dive that sent a searing stew of flame and wreckage spilling across three hundred meters of frozen Gobi.

Then it was over, with the remaining MiG cooking south on afterburner and soon out of War Club range.

Five downed MiGs was a good score, but Tag's unit had taken a shellacking. Two trucks, two PCs, and one Terrapin had been destroyed. Five men were dead, and more than a dozen others wounded, several seriously. Worst of all, Tag was certain that the Chinese would be back. This was too big a cache to lose to a single armored patrol.

Tag ran the area in the No Slack Too, directing Terrapins into position and checking on his wounded. He ordered two of the damaged vehicles that were still operable back to the bivouac with the dead and wounded. Then he encoded a message to Yeshev and burped it back to headquarters.

Tambur wheeled up in his Terrapin and shouted to Tag, "Tag Khan, men are ready to burmb these tanks. They wreaking gasoline already from them."

Distracted by all the details he had to command, Tag almost nodded his approval. "No, wait," he said. "We better have a look at those warheads first, Tambur. And I want a full inventory of the vehicles and the ordnance on them. *Then* we torch the joint. Get your people away from everything until I give the word."

"Unnerstan," said Tambur, and he sped off in his Terrapin.

Tag ordered Giesla to within fifty meters of the ammo dump, where he got out, and calling for Titz to come with him, went to inspect the crated warheads.

There were three distinct classes of ordnance in the dump. Stacked in open-sided crates were two different kinds of warheads, one olive drab, the other sky blue. The blue were longer than the green warheads and in two stages, divided by a plywood disc. In a separate pile were smaller, rope-handled boxes containing fuses.

Tag turned from his inspection and saw Titz tracing his finger across a brown sheet of cramped Chinese-characters stapled to one of the crates.

"What have you got there, Titz?"

"Bad vibes, lurchy surf. This stuff is poison, Captain Khan."

"Poison? What does it say?" Tag turned sideways between the crates and hurried to Titz's side.

"It's directions," Titz said, "how to put these two parts together and all the bongo about—what is it here?—'safe health clothes' and 'medical treatment of survivors.'"

Nerve gas. The realization went through Tag like an electric shock. And he had almost let Tambur burn them.

"Titz, quick," he said, "these green ones, what do they say?"

Titz found one of the instruction sheets for the green warheads and scanned it a moment.

"Instructions are shorter," he said, "but a lot of the same safety doo-wah. Something about, uh, not restriction . . . quarantine—that's it—quarantine periods."

"Those evil motherfuckers," Tag growled.

"You know what it is?" Titz said.

"Yeah, I know, Titz. It's fucking germs, bio bombs."

Tag ripped the sheets from two crates to take back for intelligence. "Titz," he said, "start hauling those boxes of fuses outside."

Tag ran back to the No Slack Too, gave Giesla the instruction sheets, and told her to add the gas and the bio bombs to his report to Yeshev. He found Tambur and organized a work detail to clear out the fuses from the ordnance dump and pile them at the far end of the bunker, and put the rest of the men to work vandalizing the trucks and mobile launchers. They could be effectively disabled without the risk of fire and explosions so near the biochemical weapons. What's more, Tag realized that, given their importance, they would be the object of any Chinese move, so long as the Chinese were not certain that the weapons had not been destroyed. They had hurt him with the MiGs, so he would just re-bait the trap with the same cheese.

The Mongols took a Luddite's delight in gutting circuit boards, puncturing oil pans, and decapitating carburetors on the Chinese vehicles, carrying off knobs and insignia as souvenirs and pissing in the fuel tanks. Tag set a laser-detonation charge in the cairn of fuse boxes and pulled everyone out of the water course. At a distance of three-hundred meters, he had Ham lay his laser sight on the charge, and the critical variable-time fuses were just so much smoke.

Tag ordered all his remaining trucks and PCs to fall-back positions, called in the two BMPs, and arrayed his armor to cover the approaches on the water course from the south and southeast, the direction in which the wind was shifting. He put the No Slack Too and three of the Terrapins on the bank above the bunker, and sowed the rest broadcast, in scattered fighting positions to make things hard for MiGs.

Tag ordered the patrolling Terrapins to close their sectors and told the horsemen to keep sharp.

Yeshev acknowledged the after-action report, nothing more, and Tag sat waiting, wishing he had another stack of War Clubs.

11

Tag did not have long to wait. Poor communications and other plans already afoot had delayed the Chinese air retaliation, but the danger to their plans posed by Tag's attack had stirred them to feverish action. A full thirty-six hours earlier than their original intent, the Chinese mounted their major ground offensive against the Mongols and their allies, a push across the entire front designed to draw the allies into the open, where they could be hit by the remote batteries of multiple-launch rockets—so very effective against massed armor—and by the biochemical weapons—so devastating on most living things. But the biochemical weapons were their ace in the hole, the crux of their plan. Now, they found themselves scrambling to protect that evil asset, forced into battle before they wished, despite the softening breeze that blew at their back.

The Chinese battalion of mechanized infantry sent to secure the weapons dump was supported by a dozen T-72 tanks, which led the formation, and by four lumbering, approximate clones of Soviet Hind-D helicopters, which were already approaching Tag's positions.

Tag saw the blips appear on his radar screen at almost the same moment that the muted air-alarm klaxon sounded. The speed readout told him at once that these were not MiGs.

"Four bogeys, bearing one-five-six-zero. Looks like egg beaters," Tag told his crew. He keyed the TacNet and alerted the Phalanx gunners in the Terrapins.

The heavy helicopters swept onto the scene at top speed, nearly 250 kph, and a hundred feet off the ground. At the first response of his radar detector, Tag opened fire, followed by the three Terps on the bank. The Chinese Hinds never got off a shot.

Sighting along one Hind's radar beam, Tag's robotic Phalanx churned out a twisted hawser of lead and depleted uranium that split the skin of the helicopter the way a wet rope opens flesh, tracing a line down the belly of the aircraft and peeling back a bursting seam of flames. The heavy ship could not even heel away from the Phalanx fire. Its speed carried it through the barrage and sent it crashing into the desert. It ploughed a long furrow in the soiled snow as it crumpled beneath itself and small fires popped from the edges of its collapsed underside.

The three other Hinds fared no better.

Lacking the No Slack Too's passive radar sensors, the Terrapins had to rely entirely on their closed-loop systems, which again proved their mettle. The 37mm chain guns were tailor-made for busting Hinds. One fell in the water course, smoldering for a full minute before it exploded, cooking off ordnance in screaming arcs and tattoos of tertiary explosions. The other two cleared the bank before they fell. One did manage a belly landing, skidding and twisting to a stop, before a 105mm high-explosive round from a Terrapin turned it into a funeral pyre for its crew.

Seconds after the last Hind was in flames, Tag got word that the trucks and the patrol Terrapins had reached the fallback position, and soon after that the vanguard of the Chinese column emerged on the southeast horizon.

The two BMPs that Tag had called up were fitted with racks of Russian Tree Toad antitank missiles, and he at once ordered them to the flanks of the Chinese wedge, which spread across more than a kilometer. The fields of fire from the positions on the bank and those of the rest of the Terps scattered to the south covered most of the Chinese front. Tag knew that his best hope was to cripple the armor and draw the mechanized infantry and their BRMs into his ambush at the fallback position. His Mongols had fought well up until now, but up until now they had not been asked to fight a tactical withdrawal from an ambush against an overwhelming enemy.

Tag held his breath and his fire until the lead Chinese tank was within eight-hundred meters of the water course and moving across unbroken ground.

"Shoot," he said to Ham and the Terrapin and BMP gunners simultaneously.

Ham's gunnery classes had worked. With the exception of two Terrapins that drew beads on the same target, every one of Tag's crews scored a hit on the initial volley, disabling or destroying eight of the dozen T-72s.

Tag gave the flanks and the Terrapins to the south the order to fall back, while he and the three on the bank kept the remaining Chinese occupied. The T-72s were fast enough and had 120mm guns, but their ability to fire on the run was practically nil. One irony of this was that the tanks that were merely disabled with shattered tracks or ruined engines were potentially more dangerous than the four that were now scuttering like roaches looking for a place to hide. One of the stalled T-72s fired and blasted a notch in the bank midway between the No Slack Too and the nearest Terrapin, which returned the fire to better effect, ripping the turret off the Chinese tank and nearly toppling it on its side. A plasma of fire licked from the yawning hole defined by the turret ring, A blackened arm showed itself above the flame, like that of a drowning man, then went down.

Explosions ripped the face of the bank, followed instantly by a second salvo behind them, and Tag knew it was time to hiako. Someone out there—the mechanized column was just coming into his view—had got close enough to unlimber their rocket stands. He ordered the Terrapins to take off, while he covered their retreat. Only two started from their positions, however. The third sat smoking in its tracks, its turbine grille riddled by shrapnel.

Tag ordered the men out of it and onto the skimpy foredecks of the two operable Terrapins, next to the Phalanx cupolas. He kept his guns on the Chinese until the Terps were nearly out of sight, then told Giesla to start their run.

To lure the Chinese, the No Slack Too had to cross the open water course, which was now in full view of both the remaining Chinese tanks and the advancing armored infantry. It was more than three hundred meters across the runoff basin before the land fell away again to give the XM-F4 a covering defilade, three hundred meters of running broadside to the enemy's guns.

"Ham," Tag said, "when we break into the open, it's gunner's choice. Fruits, man the Phalanx. And Gies, don't spare the horses."

Surprise and the phenomenal speed of the No Slack Too were on their side. Giesla circled down off the bank, out of sight of the Chinese, lined up the shortest leg across the wide roll of land, and cocked open both throttles. She jacked the air-torsion suspension tighter, and the XM-F4 brought its belly pan up off the snow, already notching 90 kph and gaining speed as it broke from behind the bank. The smoldering Hind gave them some additional initial cover, but less than one-third of the way across, the No Slack Too drew fire.

The muzzle flashes from two T-72s registered on Ham's heat-sensor sight a fraction of a second before the rounds bracketed them. He locked on the left-hand image, and an integral-propellant sabot roared from the tube, peeling away to send its penetrator core augering through the glacis armor of the T-72. The explosion blasted through the belly of the tank, driving it forward to a stop, seconds before the fuel cells ignited.

Ham fired his second shot through the geyser of sand, snow, and smoke thrown up by the next shot from the other tank. He never saw the fender and track carriage fly from its side, shelling treads like parched corn, never saw the black combustion of hydraulic fluids where the tank went down hard on its amputation.

Giesla cut a series of irregular tacks through a creeping flurry of antitank fire from the armored infantry, as hasty salvos of rockets fired on the run and thunderous detonations from the guns of the surviving T-72s burst all around them, rocking the No Slack Too and scouring its slick-skin armor with non sequiturs of shrapnel. At one moment, the entire world was exploding around them, and at the next they were safe, into the defile, and racing away from the advancing Chinese at 110 kph.

When the Hinds had come in, instead of MiGs, the real estate value of Tag's fallback ambush had gone way up, and he didn't want to miss the chance to show it to the Chinese. The area was no more than a hundred acres of slightly elevated land, a low, open plateau tailing off into the desert to the south. But the roll of its top offered cover from ground fire in a hundred different places, and erosion gutters on two sides formed natural tank barriers and narrow killing zones on the approaches. He ordered Giesla to bring them up the back of an *ao bao* knoll, so he could confirm that the Chinese were in pursuit.

Scanning the horizon with his optical scope, Tag could see the twists of smoke from the fight still rising, spreading a pall over the scene. A turreted BRM broke into view, then another.

"Target," Tag said.

"Confirmed," Ham replied. "Sabot or HE?"

"HE," said Tag. He heard the carousel hum. "Shoot."

"Shot," Ham said, his voice all but lost in the sound of the gun.

"Splish-slash, Hambone. Good shot," Tag said. The BRM lay on its side, oily flame lapping from a gaping hole. "Okay, here come the rest. Let's hit it, Gies."

She worked the controls and spun the No Slack Too from its perch, carrying a blur of snow on its whirling tracks.

Giesla slowed enough on this leg of their withdrawal for the Chinese to catch a glimpse or two of them, then she whipped the turbines to high whine and raced for the ambush site.

Giesla had given them enough of a lead that Tag was able to reposition some of his armor and go over the ambush plan with Tambur. If the Chinese came at them from the east or south, the most likely routes, the column had only three approaches, all of them covered by the Terrapins. Depending on how the Chinese deployed, Tag could then make last-minute adjustments and control fire from a position commanding all three. An order of withdrawal was planned for the Terrapins, to draw the Chinese deeper into the ambush after the initial blow, and Tag sent word to the men with the trucks that company was coming.

Tag could see the Chinese from three kilometers away, three columns of APCs, led by a formation of turret-equipped antitank vehicles. They had left at least part of their troops and the T-72s behind. He had spent many days in his cat-and-mouse clashes with the Chinese feeling like Custer entering Medicine Hat Coulee. Now he knew how the Indians felt at Greasy Grass, on the wide slope there above Rosebud Creek.

Tag's armor was all out of sight, behind the crests of the knolls, as was the No Slack Too, and he lay on his belly in the snow, watching the Chinese through his binoculars, waiting to see how they played the hand. They were not fools. The main body of the column scattered and halted a full kilometer from the choke points at the foot of the low plateau, and a scout detachment came forward. The six antitank BRMs prowled the area and located the approaches through the gullies, then came up them in twos and fanned out in a perimeter, investing the initial points of high ground that Tag had left unoccupied. The main body began reforming its columns and moving forward.

Tag counted fifteen vehicles in each column, totaling at least two reinforced companies of infantry. He waited until the first of them had negotiated the approaches, then scuttled back from the crest and through the commander's hatch of the No Slack Too.

He threw the dogs on the hatch, jerked a CVC on his head, and keyed the TacNet, "First units, this is Butcher Boy. Go. Go."

Giesla shot the XM-F4 forward into its fighting position. Perhaps a third of the Chinese appeared to have crossed the choke points and taken up positions, but they had not disgorged their infantry. From his commanding elevation four hundred meters away, the Chinese looked to Tag like a formation of toy soldiers. And then that neat order was shattered by the guns of the Terrapins.

Firing cannon and Phalanxes simultaneously, the tough, nimble weapons platforms, with their state-of-the-art sights and ordnance, raked the unsuspecting Chinese like the harrows of hell. Five of the six antitank BRMs went up with the first salvo, blasted from their low crests by deadly 105mm fire. A half-dozen of the troop carriers took direct, obliterating hits, and the rest had fist-size holes punched through their thin armor by the storms of slugs from the Phalanxes, mangling the men trapped inside. The APCs began to burst into flames.

The second salvo from the Terrapins finished the job and took out four more APCs still on the approaches. The main body fell back into the desert in confusion.

The Terrapins ceased their fire while the Chinese regrouped and Tag watched. He had held his fire from the No Slack Too throughout, concentrating on his command and control duties and waiting to see how the Chinese would react. So far, they had not disappointed him. Their withdrawal was not even out of cannon range, but he continued to wait, until at last he saw the majority of the surviving BRMs separate from the rest and speed off to his left, clearly swinging around to look for a flank approach.

"Blockers hold position," Tag said over the TacNet. "Reaction unit, position delta. I say again, position delta."

Two of the Terrapins held their ground, while the others fell back and followed the No Slack Too to meet the enveloping Chinese.

It took a matter of minutes for Tag's unit to redeploy to their preplanned fighting positions on the east side of the plateau. Approaching from this side, the Chinese did not have to move in column, and so had spread their front for the assault. Twenty armored personnel carriers hit the hills, and Tag let them come within a hundred meters of his guns before he gave the order to fire.

Even at that range, the Chinese had more opportunities to find cover and off-load the troops than during the initial ambush. Only six of the BRMs suffered lethal hits in the first volley. But as the others ducked behind hillocks, Tag and the Terrapins moved forward, surprising several of the APCs with only half their troops unloaded and ripping them mercilessly with Phalanx and machine gun fire. One group of BRMs that survived this onslaught raced through it and tried to form a perimeter behind Tag's unit, only to be surprised by a fusillade of ATGMs from the racks in the rear of the two five-ton trucks and screaming rounds from the recoilless rifle mounted on one of the PCs. A handful of scattered survivors turned back south again, with Terrapins in pursuit, chasing them toward the two Terps that had stayed behind.

Tag opened his hatch and stood to listen to the sounds of the running battle. There was no question who was winning.

"Butcher Boy, Butcher Boy," Yeshev's voice came over the ComNet, "this is Alpha Fox. Status report. Over."

Tag could hear the sounds of cannon in the background behind Yeshev's voice. "Alpha Fox," he said, "this is Butcher Boy. Have neutralized approximately three-zero bravo romeo mikes. Currently engaging approximately one-zero others. Over."

"Roger, Butcher Boy. Well done. Can you return to original position? Over."

"Can do, Alpha Fox. Over."

"At your best speed, Butcher Boy. Alpha Fox out."

Tag ordered the men with the trucks and PCs to sweep the plateau, with the two BMPs and the Terrapin with the ruined radio as support, while he moved the others south, back into the desert, where six of the Chinese BRMs had managed to make an escape.

Tag was irked that he had not given orders for the Terps to pursue any survivors, but since they were headed his way, it didn't seem to matter. They could only run; they couldn't hide.

Tag lost sight of the Chinese once they entered the rolling country nearer the water course, so he increased his own rate of advance. He didn't worry that the fleeing BRMs would announce his presence. He just didn't want to give the other Chinese too long to think about it.

Fruits Tutti was riding in the open hatch of the turret when he heard the sounds of fighting, heavy cannon fire and the slurred stutter of automatic weapons.

"Hey, Captain Max," he said through his CVC, "we got action up ahead. Lots of it, by da sound."

Tag slowed and ordered the Terrapins to fan out and prepare to rush the Chinese position. The No Slack Too was cresting the last of three swells when two BRMs appeared, coming toward it. Ham knocked them out in rapid succession, and Tag accelerated their pace.

He had been in a hurry for nothing. When the bank of the water course at last came in view, it was obvious that there was little if any fighting left to do. Everywhere, as more and more of the area fell under his gaze, Tag saw the flaming hulks of Chinese APCs, the fire-gutted carcasses of tanks. Between him and the killing zone there was a formation of T-80 tanks and BMPs closing in.

"Alpha Fox," Tag radioed, "this is Butcher Boy. We have you in sight and request permission to come in. Over."

"Roger, Butcher Boy. Come in. Alpha Fox out."

Tag found Yeshev in his T-80B on the bank overlooking the slaughter. The Russian was sitting on the turret, smoking a cigarette and writing in a small cloth-covered notebook.

Giesla pulled the No Slack Too up beside the T-80B, and Tag, standing up in the commander's hatch, said, "Working on your memoirs?"

Yeshev chuckled and shut the book. "Perhaps," he said. "I keep a log of all engagements."

"So," Tag said, "what's the deal? What are you guys doing here?"

"Get out," said Yeshev, "so we can talk."

Tag and Yeshev stood between their tanks, and the Russian said, "You certainly shook a hornets' nest with your foray here, Max. This morning, the Chinese attacked all across the line. We were ordered to take this position and secure the weapons you found, and it is good that we did. The Chinese were already reinforcing when we arrived, but I think they did not expect us, as you can see." He gestured toward the acres of mangled Chinese armor and the litter of dead bodies below. "I take it that the rest of your operation went well."

"Right as rain," said Tag. "There may be a few strays still running loose, but they don't want any part of us."

A formation of six MiGs wailed past at low altitude, causing Tag to flinch.

"They are ours," said Yeshev, shaking another cigarette from his pack. "We established our air dominance within the first hour. The Chinese are already falling back."

"Do we have any new orders?"

"No . . . and yes," Yeshev said. "We hold our position here until the disposal unit arrives. Then, we return to bivouac and break camp. We are through here, I think, Max."

Tag was stunned. "Just like that?" he said. "Just like that, and it's over?"

Yeshev blew a thick cloud of smoke. "Yes, I think so. I think the Chinese hoped to win by a lightning strike. But that has not happened. No, now they would have to expose themselves too long, allow the full range of our arsenals to be brought to bear. I am sure our fliers would enjoy trying their fuel-air bombs on Chinese in the open."

"Yeah," Tag said, "that would be a real Chinese stir-fry. But you say it won't happen?"

Yeshev shrugged. "There is always the possibility of a counterattack, but not, I think, this year."

"How long until we're relieved here?"

"Tomorrow, perhaps. Until then, move your unit up here and secure this part of our perimeter for the night. And I would like to have my tank crew back."

Once the Terrapins were deployed, Tag contacted the units he had left on the plateau and ordered them to join the rest of the force. Then he headed out to meet them.

There was still too much adrenaline in his veins and too many Chinese at loose for Tag to really relax, but he did ride in the open hatch with a growing sense of accomplishment and pride in his crew and in the Mongols who manned the Terps. Hell, he liked the Mongols, all of them. He thought of old Hangay, riding down with his Mauser on men with AKs, to keep them from surrounding a tank, and he thought of the courage of Hangay's family and of the Mongols' joy in singing and dancing. He thought he would like to come here in the peace of spring, with a good horse, and travel the high grasslands to the north, all the way to the forests on the Siberian border.

Tag made contact with the rest of his ad hoc unit in the flat country southeast of the plateau. They had two dead and a few wounded of their own, in addition to nearly forty prisoners, most of whom were shot up.

Tag found Yuri, Yeshev's driver, in his armored jeep, and said, "How did it go back there?"

"Any Chinese that we did not find will probably die tonight," replied the Russian tanker. "And you?"

"Your boss says it may all be over by morning, but he's anxious to have you back with him. Let's get rolling."

Yeshev proved to be right, or nearly so. Night passed uneventfully for the tankers on the desert, although a shortage of fuel made it impossible for everyone to sleep warm, and by midmorning of the next day a convoy of troops and a bomb-disposal unit were on their way to relieve them. Tag and the Terrapins left for the bivouac with the slower-moving trucks, once Yeshev had word that their relief was on the way.

The men got no time off, however, back at camp. The rest of that day and part of the next were spent in feverish activity, striking tents and yurts, breaking down field kitchens, gathering up wire and mines, and generally policing the area in preparation for leaving. Yeshev and the rest of the skeleton regiment arrived in the afternoon, and word continued to filter in about the Chinese defeat and withdrawal. The three divisions that had come across the border of the two Mongolias had all been driven back, all sustaining heavy losses, except those units that had seen how things were going and embraced the better part of valor. Supported by the Russian, British, and French brigades, the Mongols had fought well and were rapidly moving on the border to seal it. There would be no incursion into Chinese Mongolia, where the five reserve divisions still presented a formidable force. With better weather coming on, and spring not far away, more reinforcements could be brought across Siberia or landed at the Siberian ports that had been icebound all winter. The Chinese window of opportunity had been shut fast.

By the time Yeshev and Tag led their units into the tank park at the military compound, the men were in high spirits, and Tag was even, momentarily, glad to see Colonel Menefee.

12

Giesla had not yet killed the turbines when Colonel Menefee appeared in the tank park with a platoon of U.S. Army technicians and another of armed soldiers and took charge of the No Slack Too and the Terrapins.

"Now ain't dis some shit?" said Fruits Tutti as he stood on top of the turret, watching the men swarm over the armor and shoo the Mongol crews aside. "We finally get some backup."

"Clear your porn mags out of the turret, Sergeant," Menefee shouted up to him. "Everything here is getting a complete technical workup. And," he said to Tag, who had just emerged through his hatch, "I'll expect you and Lieutenant Ruther at the debriefing in one hour, Max. I'll get someone to show you to your quarters."

Tag and Giesla had adjacent rooms in the BOQ, just across a parade ground from the transient barracks where Ham and Fruits were billeted, and there were apples, candy, and thermoses of tea set out for them. Tag showered and shaved and from his duffel shook out a jumpsuit that smelled relatively clean. He drank a cup of the brown tea and was ready when the runner arrived to lead him and Giesla to Menefee.

The operations room was in a bunker deep beneath one of the administration buildings, and Tag and Giesla had to descend ten flights of iron stairs before they reached a door that led into a wide concrete hallway, dimly lit by bulbs hung high in wire cages. The runner took them past three unmarked armored doors, then stopped at the fourth, tapped a series of numbers into the keypad on the jamb, and stood facing the center of the door until a buzz signaled that it was open. He held the door for Tag and Giesla and shut himself in the hall.

The room itself was better lit and full of activity. In the center, junior officers from four armies were making changes on three large contour tables and a corresponding map board. There was a steady murmur from the operators at the banks of radios, and a syncopated clack from the computer terminals that lined three walls. At one end was a briefing room, where Colonel Menefee had called the meeting.

In addition to Menefee, Yeshev, and Minski, Tag was surprised to see Colonel Barlow, the tall, black officer from Ross Kettle's staff, as well as Titz, Tambur, and a Mongol officer wearing epaulets, whom Menefee introduced as General Yenghis. The preliminaries were brief and formal, then Menefee took over, asking Tag and Giesla to recount their mission. When the narrative was complete, Colonel Barlow had some technical queries about the performance of the Terrapins, and Yeshev concluded with his own version of events and an evaluation of the Terrapins.

"Is it okay for me to ask a couple of questions now?" asked Tag.

"Like what, Max?" Menefee said.

"Like what's all the rush to get us back here? And why all those techs? That was like getting boarded by pirates, Colonel. And, for that matter, what the hell's been happening in the rest of the world? We haven't been getting much mail in bivouac."

"At ease, Max," said Menefee. "You'll get all your answers, but not right now. Right now, General Yenghis has something to say. General."

The general was a thickset man with a high forehead and a hawk nose. He smiled warmly at Tag and Giesla as he spoke, pausing conveniently for Titz to translate. He praised them for their courage and skill, and said he was, in Titz's translation, "bowled over" by how they had touched the hearts of the Mongol people and the soldiers. There would be a celebration to honor them that evening, after they had rested.

Tag looked at Giesla, and she rolled her eyes.

"Max," said Colonel Barlow, "I think I can probably tell you what you want to know. But trust me: everything can wait a few hours. Have a beer, take a nap. Relax."

Tag smiled and said, "That sounds like an order to me, sir."

Menefee took Tag and Giesla to an elevator, unlocked its controls with a key on his belt, and carried them to the ground floor of the building above.

"My office is just down the hall," said Menefee, "number 104. Check in the cabinet to the right of the desk."

He shut the elevator door, and Tag could hear the hum of machinery carrying it back into the earth. Menefee's office was unlocked and almost bare inside—no papers in view, not even a pencil or rubber band, and no computer terminal—but in the supply locker Menefee had described there were a dozen bottles of German beer, twelve different kinds.

"Sometimes," said Giesla, "sometimes I think your Colonel Satin Ass is truly human."

"Smoke and mirrors, darling. Smoke and mirrors."

Back at the BOQ, Tag and Giesla found a VOA popular-music program on the shortwave, pried the lids off two of the assorted beers, and stretched out on the single bed in his suite, both of them feeling the wisdom of rest in their bones.

"What are you thinking, Max?" Giesla asked.

Tag swallowed and said, "I was just wondering about Barlow. Something is up, Gies—we both know that—and

I don't think Barlow would be here if, A, it didn't involve Kettle and us directly, and, B, if it wasn't happening damn fast."

"Europe again, you think?"

"Your guess is as good as mine."

"But must it be bad news?"

Tag drained his bottle, set it on the floor, and picked up a fresh one. "Well, if history is any lesson, I wouldn't bet against it."

Giesla belched contentedly and handed him her empty.

"Give me another beer, then," she said. "Can we both sleep in this bed?"

"If you don't kick," he said, handing her a beer.

"I only kick when you snore."

"Or when I tickle you."

Giesla took a drink. "Max," she said, staring straight ahead, "if you do, you will never father children. I am warning you."

Tag could resist anything except temptation, but when he twisted to go for her ribs, Giesla spewed him with a mouthful of warm beer, and then they were tasting it again on each other's lips, exchanging a long, yeasty kiss that left them both in breathless laughter, with Tag nearly falling from the narrow bed.

"You drunk!" said Giesla. "Go shower off that smell."

"I may need a hand, so I don't stagger and fall," Tag said, pulling on her wrist.

Giesla turned and sat on the edge of the bed. "Poor man," she said, unzipping her jumpsuit.

They left their clothes in piles and went naked into the bathroom. The shower was a dreary concrete stall, but it was large, and there seemed to be an unlimited supply of very hot water that poured from a brass sprinkler in the ceiling. They soaped each other with their hands, each lingering over the other's body, finding joy and sadness in the memories of the scars.

There was the welt high inside Giesla's thigh, from the wound she had received when they first met, in the first days of Firebreak, Europe's Third World War. For both of them, it brought recollection of her brother, Tag's friend, Frederich Holz, who had died leading the Jagd Kommando unit that saved Tag and his men when they were trapped behind the Soviet line. And it brought back the memory of that first time they made love, in the barn loft in southern Germany, amid the crashing of a thunderstorm, less than twelve hours before the critical encounter with the Soviet antitank patrol that sprang the original No Slack free.

Giesla trailed her fingertips lightly over the ugly, puckered patch on Tag's shoulder, memento of his battlefield encounter with Yeshev and reminder of Wheels Latta, the No Slack Too's first driver, who died in the same ambush that wounded Tag.

Friends. Family. Pieces of themselves.

They made slow, soapy, yearning love standing up in the shower, then slept curled like two children on the bachelor's bed, until a knock at the door awakened them at 1730, and a runner announced that there would be a car for them in an hour.

The old Russian Volga sedan was clattery and had a weak heater, but the car was less a necessity than an honor, for it carried them only as far as the quadrangle of the compound, where one side was dominated by a building with a peculiar facade, like some architectural hybrid of a tantric temple and Red Square. It was the base theater, although it lacked fixed rows of seats and a sloping floor, which made it perfect for the rows of tables and chairs laid for the banquet. There were flags and flowers on the stage, and a low dais set beneath it among the other tables, most of which were already full. A Mongol usher bid Tag and Giesla follow him to the front of the room, where they joined Yeshev, Menefee, and Minski at General Yenghis's table. Ham and Fruits sat nearby with Yuri, Dmitri, and Zig from Yeshev's crew.

In the center of each table sat a smoking brass hot pot—a lantern-shaped chimney surrounded by a trough of water kept boiling by the smoldering coal inside. Around the hot pot was a lazy susan set with plates of sliced mutton, bowls of glass noodles, raw greens, sweet garlic stems, vinegars, sauces, pots of yogurt, baskets of hard barley bread, clean plates, and chopsticks.

As waiters brought beer and wine and tea, Yenghis went to the microphone on the dais and spoke briefly, gesturing toward his table, then led the applause before sitting down.

From his time in Beijing, Yeshev was familiar with the Mongolian hot pot, and was pleased to show the others how to cook the meat and noodles and vegetables in the boiling moat and mix condiments for them from the cruets and pots on the revolving ring—all with chopsticks. Yenghis laughed good-naturedly at Tag's clumsiness and gallantly helped Giesla to some choice cuts of sheep, maintaining a convivial dignity that Tag was beginning to recognize as characteristic of the Mongols. He thought it said something that the communal, gregarious hot pot, a nomad's camp stove, still held the place of honor at a general's banquet.

The main courses ended with Yenghis dipping the soupy water from the trough into bowls and passing them to everyone to drink. Then the waiters cleared and brought cookies and fruits, tea, coffee, and plum brandy. A band consisting of a guitar, a moon lute, a large and a small two-string fiddle, and a thing on legs that looked like a hammer dulcimer, began to tune up on the dais.

The song winner from bivouac got up and yowled, all stylized and operatic, an orchestrated version of the "Ten T'ousman Victimy" that ran more than ten minutes. Then a woman in an army jacket, but wearing a beaded felt skirt and black riding boots, came to the microphone and sang ballads, including one Tag recognized as "Meet Me at the *Ao Bao.*"

An orderly came and whispered in Yenghis's ear, and he rose and stepped to the dais, motioning the singer aside. Tag, who had been ignoring the music as best he could, was talking to Giesla about the metaphysical implications of the hot pot and almost missed the English name Yenghis used.

Tag looked up and followed the Mongol general's eyes to the back of the room. Yenghis barked something over the microphone, and the room stood to attention as a party of American officers entered from the rear, led by the wiry figure of General Ross Kettle.

Kettle was not tall, but he had the long legs and rolling gait of a horseman, and were it not for his amber eyes and pale hair shading into gray, he might have passed for a Mongol himself. He certainly looked in profile like a brother to Yenghis as he approached and shook hands with him. The woman who had been singing came to the table and translated greetings, then followed Yenghis and Kettle back to the microphone, where the Mongol general said a few more words before Kettle stepped to the mike, along with the translator, and said, "Please, sit down. This is a party, not a briefing. Would someone get me a beer?"

The translation brought a laugh from the Mongols and a round of applause.

"I am sorry I'm late," Kettle continued, following a drink of beer, "because this is a very special celebration, to honor some very brave, resourceful soldiers, at the conclusion of a very dangerous and crucial operation. And more than that, at the beginning of a new epoch in world history. Entire armies that were, only months ago, mortal enemies in the field have come together here in support of a mutual friend, against a common enemy. That enemy is not China, or not China alone; it is aggression, the greed for power, and the debasement of culture. It is tyranny, in whatever guise it assumes.

"In this cause, I am especially proud of the actions of those forces under my own flag, particularly of the training and development unit commanded by Colonel Roger Menefee and led in the field by Captain Max Tag . . ."

This brought applause and shouts of "Gar!" from the Mongol Terrapin crews.

" . . . and of the troops who served with them. You have written new chapters in history and in the textbooks of military science.

"Now, let us celebrate this moment and the brave men and women who have given it to us."

Kettle raised his glass of beer, and the entire room drank a toast. The band struck up a quarter-tone rendition of "Gerry Owen," and Kettle returned to the table, where Barlow and another colonel had already taken seats.

After the round of greetings and amenities, Tag said to Kettle, "You've come an awfully long way to make such a short speech, sir."

"Oh, I'll have a little more to say at the awards ceremony tomorrow, Max. I believe I have three boxes with your name on them."

"What's that, sir?" Tag said. "What awards?"

"Didn't Colonel Menefee tell you?" said Kettle. "The DSC, a Silver Star, and a cluster for your Purple Heart, all for action last year in Europe, but this seemed a good time and place for the decoration. Lieutenant Ruther and Sergeants Jefferson and Tutti will also be in the line, Max, and I believe that General Yenghis has ordered a Mongol decoration. It should be quite a show."

"I'm honored, sir—we all are," said Tag, "but surely the general didn't come all the way here just for that. I mean . . ."

"You mean," Kettle said, "what does it mean for you?"

"Yes, sir. That too," Tag said. "But also, does this mean things have reached a point in Europe where you don't *have* to be there? I know that we're two months out of touch, but when we crossed Russia, there were still military hostiles working out there."

"Yes, Max," Kettle said, "things have changed quite rapidly. Eastern Europe remembers the freedom of the nineties. There have been elections, trials, a few riots, but mostly a pell-mell stampede back to democracy. And in Russia it has been overwhelming. The Democratic Workers Party has come out on top again, Svetlov's constitution has been reinstated, and Ford and Fiat are already back in business. The two big problems now are economic restructuring and radiation pollution."

"How bad is it, General Kettle?" asked Giesla. "The radiation problem, I mean."

Kettle looked very sad. "Most of the southern part of your country, Lieutenant, between Bavaria and the Black Forest, will be uninhabitable for the rest of this century, as well as small areas of France and Switzerland. There are some fifty thousand civilians dead from the atomic exchange, and two hundred thousand more with varying degrees of radiation poisoning. Scientists are still sorting out the peripheral effects. It is bad."

Giesla merely nodded.

"So what is NATO doing, sir?" said Tag.

"Soon, they'll be doing without me, Max," Kettle replied.

"What?" said Tag and Giesla at once.

"That's right," Kettle continued. "I've asked to be relieved as SACEUR. They need an administrator in there now. Besides, Europe is no longer where the action is."

"So, where will the general be going?" said Tag.

"That, in part, involves you, Max, as well as Colonel Menefee. I'd like you both, along with Lieutenant Ruther, to join me for coffee in my quarters, after we leave here."

Following the singing, General Yenghis made another short speech and left the theater with Kettle, and then the party broke up.

Menefee rode with Tag and Giesla in the cold Volga to the VIP quarters where Kettle was staying. He and Barlow were waiting in the sitting room of the suite when Tag and the others arrived. They helped themselves to coffee from a silver service and settled into the couch and chairs. Kettle packed tobacco into a gnarled briar pipe, examined it, then fired the bowl with a butane lighter, before he spoke.

"In less than one year," he began, "we have changed the course of history. I cannot say that there will never be another massive confrontation such as the war in Europe or what nearly occurred here, but not, at least, for many years. No, what we must face now, the danger that still exists to world peace, will be found in regional conflicts in strategic areas of the globe. We have seen it many times before, when small, prosperous states have become the objects of envy or greed for larger, more aggressive neighbors. We have seen it in Europe, Latin America, Asia, the Middle East, and we are seeing it still.

"With the world's attention consumed by the war in Europe, many of these hot spots of conflict have flared to open aggression, but the public revulsion for war right now would never condone a major military expedition, such as the one launched against Iraq in the early nineties.

"With this in mind, the United States Military Assistance Command, acting on a proposal and request that I submitted, has agreed to participate in an international brigade, composed primarily but not entirely of NATO allies, whose function would officially be advisory and educational. That brigade will be under my command, and I want all of you involved."

"Sir," said Tag, "you said it would be *officially* advisory and educational—is there more?"

"Quite a bit more, Max," said Kettle, "but we're still

working out a lot of the details, don't even have a command structure yet. Suffice it to say, the experience you have gathered during the past seven or eight months will not be put to waste. The success of, first, the XM-series tanks, and now of the Terrapins, has also opened floodgates in the congressional budget committees. There's going to be a lot of R and D work for all of you, before we ever take to the field. Those Terrapins that you brought out here were only first drafts, you know, but they are the only ones in existence."

"So that's why all the technicians and guards," said Tag.

"That's right, Max," said Barlow. "We're doing an initial R and D evaluation right now, tonight."

"So, when do we go back to work?" Giesla asked.

"We're not quite finished here yet, Lieutenant," said Menefee. "There's at least a couple of days of paperwork. After that, I want you two to accompany the Terrapins back to Germany by rail."

"And then?" Tag asked.

"Then," said Kettle, "I've arranged for forty-five days of leave for all of you, Sergeants Jefferson and Tutti included, to give you all time to get to Fort Hood. By that time, we should have something more specific in mind. I can count on you, then?"

"Yes, sir," said Tag.

"Good," said Kettle, exhaling a cloud of pipe smoke, "I will see you all at the ceremony in the morning."

The medal presentations were held on the quadrangle in front of the theater, under a clear blue sky, with a cool breeze blowing. Kettle read the citations and pinned the Silver Stars on Tag and each member of his crew, followed by Tag's DSC, and the cluster for his Purple Heart, and then Yenghis hung elaborate medallions around their necks and presented them with red-and-gold sashes.

By noon, Menefee had them back in his spartan office, poring over paperwork. Yeshev came to say good-bye and tell them that he would be staying with his unit in

Mongolia, instead of returning to Russia.

"You see, Max," he said, "they cannot do with us or without us. But I think this is only a penance. Perhaps we will meet again, when I am rehabilitated." Yeshev smiled wryly.

Tag shook his hand. "I hope so, Feyodr," he said. "You were a formidable enemy, but you are a better ally, a better . . . friend."

"Yes, my friend," said Yeshev, releasing Tag's hand. "Good luck to you."

"And to you," said Tag.

Ham and Fruits stopped by later in the afternoon, to have their travel orders signed by Menefee. They were flying out the next morning, bound for home via Germany. They arranged to meet with Tag and Giesla later for a farewell drink at the BOQ.

When Ham and Fruits arrived at his quarters, Tag had broken out the bottle of bourbon that Barlow had given him, and the three of them were getting tight when Giesla came in through the adjoining door.

"Here's to Our Lady of Armor," said Fruits.

She hugged him and Ham and took a glass of whiskey from Tag.

"To all of you and all of us," she said.

They four drank and talked and danced to music on the VOA until the bottle was empty, and Ham and Fruits said their good-byes.

Giesla and Tag spent many long hours over the next three days composing a complete after-action report and helping the people in intelligence sort out the data they had gathered. The technicians, meanwhile, had gone through every system, electronic and mechanical, on the No Slack Too and the Terrapins, before declaring them ready for transport. On the morning of the fourth day, Tag and Giesla rode with Menefee in the old Volga to the rail yard in the compound.

"I'll be flying out in the morning myself," said Menefee, "and I'll meet you in Germany. Between now and then, I hope you enjoy your trip. And be sure to look at the bedside reading I left for you."

"Thank you, sir," said Tag, uncertain whether he heard any sarcasm in the colonel's voice.

The car they boarded put an end to that question. It was one of the old Russian coaches, designed for a general or some other VIP. It contained a sitting area and a sleeping compartment and a full bath, all done in old woods, brass fixtures, and lush upholstery. There was a stereo deck and dozens of laser discs of classical music, a VCR and several movies, even a small library.

While they were putting away their gear in the sleeping compartment, Giesla opened the drawer of a table by the bed and took out a book.

"Oh, my," she said. "I think this is something that General Kettle didn't tell us."

"What's that?" said Tag.

She handed him the book.

"Oh, shit," he said. "Guess where we're headed?"

The title read, *Thirty Days to Better Arabic*.

SWAMPMASTER

They crawled up from the radioactive garbage of America's second Revolution. The armed enemies of freedom, they swarm across occupied Florida like a fungus. The enslaved masses fear them. The lucky few escape them. One man defies them . . .

His name is John Firecloud. A Native American trained by an ancient shaman in the ways of survival—and armed with a graphite compound bow—he leads a fight-or-die quest for blood and honor in a post-nuke America gone straight to hell. The swamps are his battlefield. His mission is freedom. His methods, extreme . . .

*Turn the page
for a sample
of this exciting new series,
coming from Diamond Books
in February.*

Firecloud pressed a finger to the protective medicine pouch of *aha lvbvkca* and cedar leaves hung from his neck, and uttered a silent prayer to gods he scarcely believed in anymore.

He ran the fingers of his other hand down the smooth, curved fiberglass and graphite limb of the compound bow slung over his shoulder. Eight steel-tipped broadhead arrows nosed out of the snap-on quiver.

Their lethal sting was something in which he had *absolute* faith.

His decision made, Firecloud climbed off his perch and went scrambling down the tree trunk. This time he didn't need the fluttery murmur of the leaves to conceal the sound of his movement. The descending copter made racket enough.

His feet quietly touched ground moments before the acne-scarred man reached the trees.

The trooper stood whistling before a tall red mangrove whose twining prop roots snaked aggressively toward the sandbelt. He had not been in a good mood, but a sense of imminent relief had improved it—that and simply being off the beach. He hadn't really thought anyone would be scoping him if he took a leak down there; at least not anyone who mattered. The thing was, he hadn't wanted to watch the copter land. Because watching it land made him think about having to board it in just a few minutes. And when he so much as thought about boarding it, his stomach rolled as if it were already struggling with gravity.

If he'd told Vic that, Vic might have gotten the impression that he was some kind of wimp. Which was far from the case, as the Indian woman could attest. He had showed her just what kind of man he was when they'd broken into the clapboard shack she had been living in. Yeah, he'd gotten her underneath him and showed her, and it had been fine.

A justifiable hatred—not a fear, oh no; if anyone ever suggested it was some kind of irrational fear, he would beat that person to a pulp—of flying did not make him a coward. Man, he believed, had not been meant to fly. Birds flew. Goddamned bugs flew, which was why they had been given wings. Human beings did not have wings. Because they were not meant to fly. Simple logic.

He loosened his Sam Browne belt, unzipped, and began extricating himself from his pants.

He never finished.

Without warning, a hand shot out from behind and clamped over his mouth, its thumb and forefinger pinching shut his nostrils. Simultaneously another hand came around and gripped his throat. He was pulled backward, off balance. He tried to breathe, tried to scream, could do neither. His air was cut off, he was choking. His feet flailed, heels skidding on the mushy ground. He brought his own hands up and pried frantically at the arms wrapped around him. His nails bit into them but they wouldn't unlock. Their muscles bulged. The powerful fingers gripping his throat tightened. His Adam's apple was being crushed. His windpipe was swelling shut. Blood rose into his mouth, filled it, rose into his nose. The pressure in his head was enormous. He was drowning, drowning in his own blood. A haze fell over his vision. Red at first, then shot with black. Then the haze became a solid wall of black.

Just before the end he made a desperate attempt to beg for his life but could only manage a tiny, sputtering sound.

Then he went limp.

John Firecloud let the body spill out of his arms.

Blood spouted from its nostrils and gaping mouth as it crumpled into a mesh of prop roots.

Firecloud looked at the soldier and noticed the spreading wet stain on the crotch of his half-fallen pants. Death had robbed him of whatever dignity he'd possessed . . . just as he'd robbed it from the woman.

Still doesn't make them even, Firecloud thought.

He turned and watched through the trees as the Strikehawk banked for a landing. It hovered about ten feet above the ground for several moments, the wash of its rotors whipping up a funnel of sand, then settled gently onto its landing gear.

The men on the beach approached the chopper cautiously while its slowing blades beat lazy circles in the air, their captive trailing along behind.

Firecloud nocked an arrow into his bow and waited. The helicopter had come down with its starboard side to him, which meant he would be out of the pilot and co-pilot's direct line of sight. A lucky break. Now if he could only have another . . .

Upper and lower doors opened on the Strikehawk's fuselage like a square, robotic mouth.

His breath catching, Firecloud anxiously peered inside.

And got his second break.

The cabin was vacant; even the big 7.62 sidegun was unmanned. One of the men in the cockpit must have opened the doors remotely.

Firecloud exhaled with a grateful sigh. He had counted on the Strikehawk having a reduced crew since cabin space was needed to accommodate the ground patrol and their captive. But even a third of its maximum troop complement would have been sufficient to make him a vastly outnumbered goner. That there was no one aboard besides the flight crew was a discovery which exceeded his best hopes. Possibly the absence of any effective threat to their occupation had resulted in a slackening of the Front's military procedures.

The odds were still four-to-one against Firecloud, but he felt that he at least had a fighting chance.

He readied the bow for firing, testing its draw.

Watching. Waiting.

Inertia had finally brought the Strikehawk's blades to a halt. The aircrew had popped their windscreen canopy and the co-pilot was outside the front of the craft having a cigarette. The man named Vic and the other foot soldier had lead the Seminole woman aboard, after which Vic had emerged from the copter alone, walked slowly over to the co-pilot, and grubbed a smoke off him.

The two of them talked and puffed while in the cockpit the pilot undid his safety harness and relaxed with his helmet visor up, stretching his arms, occasionally joining in on the conversation.

Several minutes later the co-pilot stubbed his cigarette into the sand and gazed over at the trees. He said something to Vic, who turned in the same direction.

"Ray, you done yet?" he shouted, taking a last drag off his cigarette and flicking away the butt.

His only response was silence.

Firecloud added a little more tension to the bowstring.

Vic looked at the co-pilot and wagged his head, a prosy grin on his face. "Guy's bladder must hold more water than Lake Michigan," he remarked. He cupped his hands over his mouth and looked back at the trees. "Yo, Ray! You playing with yourself in there or what? We gotta take off before the bad weather hits!"

There was another parcel of silence broken only by the rhythmic slap of the waves and the cries of the gulls that had flocked inland before the advancing stormfront.

Vic's grin dwindled. "Bet he went and took a catnap, damned if he ain't sawing wood," he grumbled, shaking his head with greater annoyance. "I'll go and fetch him."

Firecloud heard more than a trace of the South in the tone and cadence of his voice. He wondered briefly if the man was a native of Florida; there were many collaborators, a percentage of whom had become full-blown National Front recruits.

Vic started quickly up the loose-packed sand toward the ridge less than thirty yards away.

Firecloud let him walk for ten yards, then took aim and fired.

An instant after the arrow whooshed from the bow he saw Vic stagger backward and look down at the shaft suddenly jutting from his chest, his face clenched with agony and utter bafflement.

He looked back at the trees with that same pain-wracked, stunned expression, opened his mouth as if to shout, and wheezed out a foam of blood and saliva.

His hands gripped the arrow and tried to pull it free, but only succeeded in further mauling the lung in which its tri-bladed head was imbedded. A scarlet flower bloomed in the center of his service blouse.

He gagged, pale pink blood bubbling over his lower lip and chin, and swayed forward.

Firecloud was off and running across the strand before Vic's face smacked the ground.

For a moment neither the pilot nor co-pilot could grasp what was happening. They stood watching with frozen, wide-eyed incomprehension as the man with the bow dashed toward them.

Then the co-pilot snapped back to awareness, looked desperately around for cover, and broke for the chopper's open passenger door.

Firecloud let him go. It was vital that he deal with the pilot next. If the man in the cockpit pulled down the armored canopy then he would be sealed off from attack.

As if reading Firecloud's thoughts, the pilot reached for the raised windscreen panel above his head.

He was a slice of an instant too late. Firecloud had halted less than fifteen feet from the chopper and loaded his bow. His firing hand a blur, he loosed the arrow, slipped another from the quiver on the bow's handgrip, and fired it in rapid succession.

Had the pilot's helmet visor been down he might have lived a bit longer. But it wasn't, and he didn't.

The tip of the first arrow ripped into his exposed right cheek and plowed an exit wound through the left. Gaudy fletching protruded from a face that immediately stretched around the shaft like a distorted funhouse mirror-image.

The second arrow drove home just as the pilot reflexively turned, gaping, toward his assailant. It socked into his right eye and burrowed deep into his head, throwing him spread-eagle backward across the cockpit.

His legs jerked twice then ceased to move.

Firecloud narrowly scrutinized the corpse for a moment, his lips compressed into a grim, tight line. He'd halved the odds against him. The Strikehawk was brain-dead.

A fighting chance, yes.

He raked his glance over his shoulder toward the cabin entrance.

And saw the surviving ground trooper jump from the boarding step and come tearing at him in a low, hump-backed charge, hands wrapped around an M-16. The co-pilot was in the sidegunner's station, calling to the soldier at the top of his voice.

"Come back, you idiot, I can't get a shot off with you in the way!" he shouted from the copter. "Goddamn it, I said *you're blocking my fire!*"

The soldier disregarded him. His eyes met Firecloud's with a steely, vengeful glare as, still running, he triggered a burst from the rifle.

Firecloud chucked his bow and dodged sideways just before a hail of lead riddled the ground on which he'd stood, churning up dry geysers of sand. The soldier swung his head around to see where he'd landed, pivoted toward him, triggered another volley. Firecloud managed to avoid the fire with a lightning quick tuck-and-roll.

"Gonna get you for Vic and Ray, bastard!" the soldier screamed, pivoting again to keep up with Firecloud's zigzagging scramble. His berserk grimace revealed a mouthful of crooked, decayed teeth. "I'm gonna blow your guts right out your ass!"

The gun muzzle chattered, pulverizing a mound of ocean debris. Shell fragments and chunks of seaweed and driftwood sprayed chaotically into the air.

Firecloud ducked, bellyrolled, weaved. He was tiring, losing his wind. Every muscle groaned from exertion. He had to put an end to the barrage—*fast*.

Powering to a low crouch, he launched himself at the man with the gun, barely skirting a murderous stream of bullets. Caught off guard by his sudden move, the soldier tried desperately to recover from his surprise and draw a bead.

Like the Strikehawk's pilot, his reflexes were a hair too slow and that slowness cost him his life.

Moving with a speed and fluidity that was almost balletic, Firecloud came in under the M-16's barrel and then sprang to his full height, hooking the barrel between his left forearm and bicep. At the same time he slammed the heel of his right hand against the soldier's head at a point just above the nose and between his eyebrows, shattering his glabella.

The man died instantly as jags of bone ripped through his brain. He collapsed, his finger spasming on the gun trigger and squeezing a round harmlessly into the air.

Firecloud tore the M-16 from the soldier's convulsive grasp as he fell.

The rifle felt uncomfortable in his hands.

He did not like guns. Guns made killing easy and so depreciated life.

Did not like them, but knew how to use them.

He spun around, poised to fire the M-16 at the helicopter.

The chopper's sidegun was pointing back at him. The co-pilot held it steady with his right hand. His left hand was twisted in the Seminole woman's hair.

He pulled hard on a fistful of hair and she shrieked, bending backward into him, her spine arched against his shoulder.

Firecloud fixed him in a hard cold stare.

"Go ahead, Indian, do me," the co-pilot snarled. "But you'll be doing the bitch, too. That's if I don't put you down first."

Firecloud was silent.

"I'm not sure what's happening here, but if this is over the woman, you can have her," the man in the helicopter said. "Flying the chopper's my business. She isn't. All you've gotta do is toss the gun and I'll let her go."

Sure you will, Firecloud thought, still saying nothing. He was positive that the instant he relinquished his weapon he would be as dead as the soldiers sprawled about the beach . . . and the woman would be left at the co-pilot's mercy.

Neither his dark eyes nor his rifle wavered. He took a slow step forward.

Thunder rumbled over the Gulf.

"Stay where you are, man!" The co-pilot wrenched the woman's head back again and she cried out sharply, her cheeks blotching with hectic color. "I can hurt her if I want to," he yelled. Listened to the thunder. "I can hurt her bad!"

Firecloud kept his gun leveled. Letting each second live. Noticing every movement, as the shaman, Charlie Tiger, had once taught him.

Each movement means something, the old man had said. *Observe. Then participate.*

He took another step.

"*Hold it!*" the co-pilot screamed. "Is she gonna have to catch more punishment? *Is she?!*" He pulled her hair a third time. Tears burst from her eyes and she squirmed in his grasp, causing his weight to shift.

His hand slipped back from the trigger.

Just a little.

Just enough.

"No. No more," Firecloud muttered under his breath, firing the M-16.

It went off with a blinding roar, recoil slamming its stock against Firecloud's shoulder, empty casings leaping into the air around him. Thrown suddenly clear of the girl, the co-pilot dervished toward the far wall of the cabin, his head vanishing in a grisly eruption as a half dozen slugs plowed into it at once.

A shapeless, bloody pulp from the shoulders up, the co-pilot's body rebounded off the wall and toppled to the copter's steel floor with a dull clang.